CHAPTER ONE

"I DON'T like red hair," Rae said.

"His hair's not red. It's brown." Whitney buttered a piece of toast and bit into it. "A touch of red, maybe, but that just brightens it up. I rather like that color."

"What you like is the color of his money...green and growing."

Whitney giggled. "That's the icing on the cake, isn't it!" she said, lifting her cup. "Paula, heat this up, will you? Or better still, bring me a fresh cup."

Paula dried her hands, emptied and refilled Whitney's cup while the two sisters continued to postulate.

"You needn't get your hopes up, dear heart. He's in San Diego for the polo match, not to see you."

Paula listened idly as she scrubbed the frying pan. The San Diego Polo Classic, sponsored for charity each October, had for weeks been the main topic of conversation. Now that the Vandercamp yacht was anchored at the San Diego Yacht Club and they had had a glimpse of Brad Vandercamp, who would participate, *he* was the main topic. And not because he was the so-called Prince of Polo! Like Rae said, it was his money. He was single, eligible and sole heir to the Vandercamp millions. Or was it billions?

All San Diego was agog that they were honored by his presence. At least, she corrected herself, a smile hovering on her lips, those of the elite set who would attend the polo matches and the grand balls attendant upon the event.

"But see me he will!" Whitney said, with smug certainty.

Paula, noting the gleam of conquest in Whitney's eyes didn't doubt that he would. Not that Whitney was all that beautiful. Her lips were too large, too voluptuous, and her nose...

I'm being catty, Paula scolded herself as she put away the frying pan, and went into the laundry room to sort the clothes. Whitney was fairly attractive, with that black hair and sensuous dark eyes. But mainly it was her confidence and that inviting sexuality that drew men to her. Yes, the prince will see her, and yes, Rae will be jealous, and—

"Where's that girl?" Mrs. Ashford's voice, slurred but sharp, cut into her thoughts. Paula dropped the lingerie she held and hurried to the kitchen. "Oh, there you are! Why didn't you bring my coffee to my room?"

"I'm sorry, ma'am, I thought you were still sleeping."

Mamie Ashford dropped her plump form into a chair and pressed a hand to her temple. "Oh, my poor head! How could anyone sleep with all the racket going on in this house! Can't you girls manage to cease your squabbling long enough to let your poor mother get a bit of rest!"

Her daughters apologized profusely, each insisting it was the fault of the other.

Paula placed two aspirin and a glass of tomato juice before her. "This might help, and I'll bring your coffee right away."

"Mother, I do hope you're not going to have one of your nasty migraines," Whitney said. "You know we're to go shopping today."

"Oh, sure," Rae said. "Whitney's got to get decked out for the costume ball where she plans to dazzle the prince!"

"As if you're not planning to—"

"Girls! Must you! My head... And I do feel a bit queasy. I think I'd better have something on my stomach, Paula. Bacon and maybe some of your cinnamon toast."

"Coming right up!" Paula took out the frying pan she had just scrubbed and hoped she wouldn't have to miss class again. If she could get the washing done and the beds made before twelve, she could make it. That is, if they got out of the house before Mrs. Ashford could think up something else for her to do. She hoped to goodness the migraine wouldn't stop the shopping trip.

It didn't. Three cups of coffee and a hefty breakfast did wonders. Or perhaps it was the mention of Brad Vandercamp that did the trick.

"So rich! And so British!" Mamie Ashford's eyes took on a dreamy haze. As if she was as young as her daughters, as hopeful of catching his fancy.

"And he's so good-looking," Whitney said.

"As handsome as his grandfather," her mother said. "And just as big a devil, I hear!"

"Devil?"

"The same eye for a pretty lady. One affair after another, just like the old man. Cyrus Vandercamp, his grandfather, started the family fortune with railroads. But they do say he spent a big chunk of it on that movie queen of the thirties. She was no lady, mind you! But he practically deserted his family. They tell me it was quite a shameful scandal."

Rae said she wouldn't put up with that from any man.

Whitney sniffed "Once I get his ring on my finger, Brad Vandercamp can have as many mistresses as he chooses."

Mrs. Ashford agreed that the ring was the thing. Thank goodness both her daughters were ladies and wouldn't settle for less. But she did hope the polo prince would turn out to be more like his father.

"How so?" Whitney asked.

"Not a breath of scandal about him. Seems more interested in playing with gold mines, oil wells and such than with women. He's parlayed that railroad fortune into billions. Married some Lady. Somebody whose family was poor as church mice. They say he's turned Balmour, her family's crumbling estate, into a real showplace. Lord, I'd like to see it!''

"Well, you never know." Again Whitney sounded smug. "Did you say he had an eye for a pretty lady?"

Mamie Ashford chuckled. "Yes, and that's what you are. Far prettier than any of the others, all of whom will be after him. Hadn't we better get to Mademoiselle's Boutique first? There's sure to be a rush."

They did leave in plenty of time. Paula was able to finish the laundry, clean the kitchen and tidy the bedrooms before eleven. By eleven-thirty, she had showered, dressed and was on the bus headed for the university.

Paula had dreamed of being a veterinarian for as long as she could remember. She loved animals, from the tiniest kitten to the biggest horse on the Randolph cattle ranch in Wyoming, where her father was a ranch hand and her mother the family cook. As soon as she could read she became immersed in the tales of James Herriot, the famous vet who tended the sheep and cattle on the Yorkshire moors. As often as allowed, she would tag along with a cowhand or vet who tended a sick cow or horse. She and Toby, the foreman's son, planned to marry and buy a spread of their own. He would train racehorses, and she would be a veterinarian. That dream had lasted through two years of college. Then, the next fall, Toby had fallen head over heels in love with a freshman named Cynthia, and it was as if Paula had lost an anchor she had clung to all her life. Devastated, she floundered and nearly flunked out of college.

It was her uncle Lew who had steadied her. That summer, on his yearly visit to the ranch, he had a long talk with her. "Toby's just one man among millions. Stuck on this place, you just been so close to him you never looked around. And don't forget. You've still got your dream. Toby ain't got nothing to do with your being a veterinarian. That's up to you."

He was right. That would be hers, her career, a part of her that no man could take away. She determined to have it. She threw herself into her classes, made up her failures and graduated on time. But with not enough credits for the hoped-for grant to the school of veterinary science.

Disaster struck again. Her father had a spell of illness that strained the budget, and prospects for vet school were dim. They were discussing the possibilities when Lewis Grant, her father's brother, came again for his yearly visit. He offered to pay half the monstrous tuition, but even that would not be enough.

"Guess Paula'll have to stick around the ranch this year," Hank, her father, said, "maybe be a help to her mother."

"She'd rather help you," Lew said.

Paula smiled. Of course Pop would never permit

her to go out on the range, but she was very much at home on a horse and rather liked tending the animals, had even assisted at a difficult calving a couple of times. "You're right," she said. "I would rather help Pop."

"Beats me," Lew said, "why anybody would want to be on a horse out in rough weather rather than be nice and cozy in a warm kitchen." He shook his head. "Can't understand it."

"To each his own," Paula said. She remembered that Lew had long ago deserted ranch life for the city. Any city. After much traveling and several odd jobs, he finally landed a steady one as chauffeur and handyman for a Mr. Angus Ashford of San Diego, California.

"We could manage the tuition," her mother said, returning to the main topic. "But not the room and board." The state college was a hundred miles away, over mountainous roads treacherous with snow during the long winter months.

Lewis looked at Paula. She knew he understood. "Still got that veterinary bug in your head?" he asked.

She nodded.

"Well," he said, "maybe you could come to San Diego with me and go to school there."

They stared at him. What difference would that make?

"Room and board," he said. "The Ashfords'

live-in maid just gave notice." He gave Paula a keen look. "Got any objection to a little housework?"

She grinned. "You mean like I've been doing all my life?"

"Well," he said, still studying her, "I might could get you on. I can't promise, but maybe... And the old man's a pretty decent guy. He might allow you to take time for some classes."

Paula thought about it, her spirits lifting. San Diego U. "Does the university have a veterinary school?" she asked.

"Don't know about that." He hesitated. Then his chubby face lit up. "Oh, yeah! It sure does. That's where I took the old man's collie when she had to be put down."

Paula's eyes brightened. "That would be perfect! That is, if I could get admitted."

She looked at her father, reading the message in his eyes even before he spoke. "It won't be like living in a dorm, and you'll be a long way from us."

"I'll be there to look out for her," Lew said. "Don't forget...I'm her godfather."

As Hank nodded his consent, Paula threw her arms around Lew. "Thank you, thank you, thank you! Lucky me... I've got a real honest-to-goodness fairy godfather."

Her parents laughed, but Lew frowned. "We ain't there yet. I better phone the old man. I'll pour it on thick about how my very smart niece wants to go to vet school and needs a job. He owes me. After you drive a man home and put him to bed slopping drunk a few times..."

That was how it had happened. The unknown Mr. Ashford approved of a young woman's ambition, and of course he had no objection to her arranging her work to allow time for classes. Moreover, he did have some influence. She should get her papers to the school right away, and he would contact the dean.

"Lew, you're wonderful!" Paula cried, throwing her arms around her uncle.

"Maybe you won't think so when Mrs. Ashford gets hold of you," he said. "None of the other maids have lasted more'n a few weeks. She's tough. And there's another thing," he added dubiously. "You're much too good-looking. If you could tone down a bit..." He looked at Paula as if trying to diminish her slender willowy figure, the golden curls, the alert bright blue eyes.

"What's that got to do with anything?" Paula asked.

"Well. Mrs. Ashford don't like nobody outshining her girls."

"I don't understand."

"They're...what you call it? Debs this year, pictures in the paper and everything. The old lady sets a big store 'bout them being prettier than the other ones. They're big society, you know, and she has big plans, like getting both of them hooked to some big shot that's loaded."

"For goodness sake, that's nothing to do with me. I'd be the maid. I surely wouldn't be hobnobbing with them!"

"Right," Lewis assented, but he still looked dubious. "Anyway, I'm glad you got hired sight unseen."

Angus Ashford's influence got her admitted that fall, and against his wife's wishes, Paula was allowed to arrange time for classes. She was grateful and worked hard during early morning hours and sometimes late at night so nothing was left undone. Even Mrs. Ashford began to rely on her.

But when Mr. Ashford's liver gave out and he died a year after she had been there, Paula was afraid Mrs. Ashford, who had not fully taken to her, would dismiss her.

However, fate intervened. It turned out that Angus Ashford had not only been more of an alcoholic than his wife, he had also been an inveterate gambler and an unwise investor. With the death of her husband, Mrs. Ashford found that her income was somewhat reduced. She had to rid herself of the gardener and the woman who came once weekly for the wash and heavy cleaning.

Mrs. Ashford was inclined to be a bit silly, but she was no fool. She knew who would and who would not willingly do it all. She retained Lewis as chauffeur, gardener and handyman. Paula became the cook, washwoman and maid. All with very little increase in salary.

Paula didn't complain. She was used to hard work. *I'm just lucky I didn't have to drop any classes,* she thought that afternoon, as she joined her group in the chemistry lab.

As she was leaving class, Link, one of the boys in her lab group, caught her arm. "Hey, Paula, some of us are going over for a little volleyball and then to the Hut for some pizza. Want to come along?"

"Oh, Link, I'd like to, but I don't have time. I'm sorry," she said.

"Jeez, you never have time," Link complained as he moved off with the gang.

Paula looked after them with longing. But what could she do? She had to get back in time to make dinner.

She couldn't seem to still the sense of longing. It was intensified that evening after dinner when the Ashford women displayed all the outfits purchased that day. The black linen Whitney would wear at the match, the outfits and fancy masks for the costume party, and turquoise chiffon, sure to be a hit at the final ball.

"That color does so much for my eyes, don't you think?" Whitney focused her sultry eyes on Paula. "But you'll have to tuck in the shoulders a bit. Not too much." She giggled. "Wouldn't want to spill that cleavage that's going to knock *him* out!"

Rae tried to get in a word as Whitney preened

before the mirror. "Do you like this blue on me, Paula? And will you do my hair for the dance? You know, like you did last week!"

Paula praised and promised and tried not to be envious. But the next day, as she made the tuck in the turquoise chiffon, her fingers lingered over the soft material. She had never in her life owned such a dress. How would it look on her?

Well, why not see! While they were out buying more. What harm would it do?

Quickly she shed her jeans and shirt. Stepped into the soft folds and zipped it up. It was too big and too long, but she gathered the dress about her and preened as Whitney had.

She brought her face close and peered into the mirror. Did it do something for her eyes? She tried to look sultry.

No good. Her eyes were too big.

But they did take on that color, didn't they? She bet if she went to the dance and *he* looked at her, *his* eyes would melt into hers, and they would dance and dance and...

Oh, for goodness sake, she'd best stop twirling around. If she tore that dress there'd be hell to pay.

And why was she standing here, wasting time? She couldn't afford such a dress, and, even if she could, where would she wear it? She wasn't going to any ball, and she certainly wasn't going to dance with *him*. And why was she thinking of him, anyway. He wasn't a real prince. Not that she gave a darn if he was.

She took off the dress and went back to work.

When she had first come to San Diego, Paula had signed up with a caterer. She was often on her own in the evening and could earn a little extra money serving at a catered affair. She was putting away as much as she could for the time when she might enter veterinary school. But with the extra work at the Ashfords,' she hadn't had much time for other jobs.

"I'm not sure I can make it," she told Harry, the caterer, when he called, wanting an extra hand for the Moody costume party. "The Ashfords will be attending, and she likes me to help them get dressed."

"That's okay. Aren't they going to some dinner first? Everybody is."

"Yes, they are," Paula said, remembering.

"Well, then, that gives you time. I don't care if you're a little late. Please, Paula, I really need you."

"Can't you get somebody else this time?"

"Then I've got the problem of a uniform." The caterer was persnickety about uniforms and had had Paula fitted for one.

"Well..." Paula felt guilty about the uniform, and the caterer did pay well. "All right," she said, though she didn't want to go. She was tired.

But that night, as she stood in the Moodys' oversize pantry arranging hors d'oeuvres and setting out clean glasses, she didn't feel at all tired. Somehow, the gala party mood seemed to revive her. She was fascinated by the colorful costumes of the masked figures that talked, laughed and danced to the beat of the band. The scintillating music penetrated the thick walls of the pantry and seeped into her fun-starved heart. She threw back her head, humming the melody, her feet tapping in perfect rhythm as she danced around the table.

She did not hear the door open and was unaware that he watched.

"Perfect. Beautiful. But must you dance alone?" The deep voice startled her.

She stopped in her tracks. Despite the mask, she recognized him immediately. He was more handsome than in the newspaper, and his hair was like copper. "Oh, I'm sorry," she muttered, feeling humiliation flood her cheeks. "I was... I... Can I help you?" she asked.

"Indeed you can." He held out his arms. "May I have this dance, fair lady?"

She tried to laugh. "No. Sorry, but I'm not a guest. I work here."

"Oh? Well, let's fix that." The amber eyes that showed through his mask glittered with mischief. From somewhere he produced another mask and tied it over her face. "There. Now you're my guest. Shall we dance?"

She couldn't resist. He drew her to him, and for a long time she was only aware of the feel of his arms about her, the pleasant fresh smell of aftershave and the gentle firmness of his guidance as the music swelled around them. She followed his lead with easy grace, abandoning herself to the joy, reveling in the colorful pageant, the dance.

From somewhere an old grandfather clock intoned the midnight hour. The music stopped, and someone shouted, "Masks off!"

Dear Lord, she was in the middle of the ballroom!

The man bent toward her, his hand cradling her neck, his lips lightly touching hers. "Time to unmask, little one."

The slender gold chain of her necklace snapped as she fled.

CHAPTER TWO

"HEY, wait!" Too late. She had slipped through the crowd and vanished. All that was left of her was a slender gold chain dangling from his fingers. Feeling strangely bereft, he started after her. She would be in that room where—

"Brad Vandercamp, take off that disguise!" The daughter of his host blocked his way. She tugged at his mask. "You didn't fool anybody, anyway. We all knew you."

"Oh?" He looked at the costume that hugged her figure and glittered with sequins in the shape of fish scales. "Well, my little mermaid," he said trying to remember her name, "some of us are not as clever as—"

A sultry voice interrupted. "No matter how clever, you couldn't hide that copper hair."

"No more than you could hide those eyes." Sensuous and suggestive, he thought.

Whitney gushed with pleasure. "So you knew me! Tell me, are my eyes distinctive?"

"Indeed they are. They're, er, so...so expressive," he said, thinking of the last dance. She had been as light as a feather in his arms, and her blond curls had a fresh soapy scent, more tantalizing than any perfume. He must see her again, ask—

"Come along." The mermaid took his arm. "Let's have a refreshing drink. They'll be serving breakfast in a few minutes."

She will be serving, he thought, as he was borne off between the two women.

Breakfast, however, was served buffet-style, with several well-groomed waiters attending. No sight of long slender silk-clad legs beneath a short maid's costume. No sight of merry blue eyes and golden curls topped by a frilly bit of lace.

"You don't have a thing on your plate. Here, try this." The woman with the eyes popped a small sausage into his mouth. "Like it?" He nodded, and she piled more on his plate. "There. Now what kind of omelet would you like?"

"Spanish!" Carl, Brad's closest friend and teammate, ordered. "Give him some of that old San Diego flavour." He punched Brad on the back and added in a whisper, "Get with us, buddy! Where's your mind?"

In the kitchen, Brad thought, as he watched the chef preparing the omelet. Was that where she was? Best not go back there asking if someone had lost a necklace and, if so, what is your name and where do you live?

Never mind. Later. He would find her. The slender gold chain rested in his pocket...like a promise.

* * *

"Nobody knows who she was, but she was dressed as a maid."

"Maybe she *was* a maid."

Paula's heart lurched, and she stopped in the hall to listen. The sisters' voices were clear as they discussed last night's ball from their adjoining rooms where they were dressing for the first game. If they even suspected...

"Don't be silly. She wasn't a maid." Rae sounded sure. "She was a guest. She had a mask on. And—" Whatever she was going to say was cut off by the shout from across the hall.

"Paula! Where's that girl!" Mamie Ashford demanded somewhat piteously.

"I'm right here," Paula said, hurrying to her. "Just lie still and allow that bromide to settle." She adjusted the pillows and replaced the ice bag. "There now. You'll feel better soon."

"My poor head. I don't see how I'll make that committee meeting."

"You'll be fine," Paula assured her. "Just rest for a little while. I'll be back in time to help you dress." She felt sorry for the always-anxious woman. Not easy on her limited budget to buy the proper outfits and maintain the proper social commitments so important to her and her demanding daughters. Seeing that she was about to fall asleep, Paula closed the draperies and tiptoed from the room.

As she emerged, Whitney called, "Paula, where's my dress?"

"Almost ready." Paula rushed downstairs to finish pressing the dress. She returned to find Rae in Whitney's room holding out two outfits.

"Which should I wear?" she asked.

Whitney didn't answer. She carefully applied eye shadow and stared dreamily into the mirror. "He said my eyes are so expressive."

"Bet he didn't look at you like he looked at her," Rae said a little spitefully. She frowned. "Who could she be? I don't remember anybody dressed as a maid, do you, Whitney?"

"Plenty of serving maids around." Whitney peered into the mirror to inspect her makeup. "Maybe one of them sneaked onto the dance floor. I wouldn't put it past that kind."

Paula gulped, but Rae answered her sister. "I told you. She was a guest. And Brad knew her very well! The way he was holding her—"

"I thought you didn't see her."

"Sylvia did. She and Rod were dancing right next to them, and Sylvia said he was staring at her like there wasn't anybody else in the room, and when he kissed her..."

Paula's breath caught as Whitney turned to glare at her sister. "Kissed her?"

"Right there on the dance floor!"

Whitney frowned, then shrugged. "Doesn't mean

a thing. Don't you read the tabloids? He's always kissing somebody."

Paula, who had gone rigid, forced herself to relax. Whitney was right. What was a kiss to Brad Vandercamp? And his kiss certainly meant nothing to her!

"Which, Paula?" Rae's question jerked her to attention. "Should I wear this or the green one?" Rae held a yellow outfit against herself.

Paula advised the green instead while Whitney continued to muse. "So Sylvia saw her. She must know who she is."

"No. She doesn't. She said when everybody started unmasking, the woman...well, it was amazing, but she just disappeared. Sylvia asked Rod if he saw her face, but he didn't. He said he was looking at her legs."

Paula winced. This kind of talk was making her nervous.

Shucks! They didn't suspect her. They probably didn't even know she had been there. They knew she sometimes worked for Harry, often at affairs they attended. But, thank goodness, they were always too absorbed in themselves to notice her. Even when, as now, she was right under their noses.

Whitney didn't even look at her when she held out the linen she had pressed.

"Here you are," she said.

Whitney glanced at the dress, shook her head. "No. Changed my mind. Bring the dusky rose with the sexy short skirt."

Paula fetched it, tied a green scarf becomingly into Rae's hair and made sure Whitney's makeup was in her bag, along with the binoculars.

As they made their way out, she heard Rae say, "He's not playing today. Do you suppose he'll be among the spectators?"

"Of course, silly. The players always watch the techniques of the other teams. He'll be there. And I'm sure he'll linger at our box. He was quite taken with me. He said my eyes..." Her voice faded, and Paula gave a sigh of relief. If she couldn't hear them talking about him, she could stop thinking about him!

She couldn't. She stared at the rumpled sheets, the discarded clothing, a dresser cluttered with lipsticks, bottles, crumpled tissues and traces of spilled powder. But what she saw was a man with unruly copper hair and eyes that glinted with mischief. He smiled at her and held out his arms. Had he really held her in a special way? Then, when he kissed her...

Had he kissed her?

Such a fleeting touch. She might have arranged it. No. No fantasy. Her lips had burned like fire.

Vividly she recalled the dream...music, voices, laughter and the tolling of a clock.

Then the kiss. Light and fleeting, yes. But it had ignited a powder keg of emotion, sending strange and exhilarating sensations exploding through her. For a moment, she was immobile.

The loud "Masks off" broke the spell and jolted her into movement, thank goodness!

She shook her head to clear it. She was far too practical to let a dream interfere with reality. Quickly erasing last night from her mind, she went to wake Mrs. Ashford. By the time Lew returned from depositing the girls, she had their mother dressed and alert, ready to be chauffeured to her committee meeting.

Paula tidied the bedrooms and baths, finished the laundry and vacuumed. Dinner was no problem, as the Ashfords were dining out. Time to retire to her little room in the attic and study.

Two hours later, she had finished the outline for her English term paper and prepared for tomorrow's chemistry test. She heard the family car coming down the drive and glanced at the clock. Almost six. That would be Uncle Lew returning, and he would be hungry. She hurried to the kitchen.

"Where's the chow?" Lew asked, as he tossed aside his chauffeur's cap and popped open a can of soda.

"Coming right up," she said. "I wasn't sure when you'd be back."

"Me, either. Been driving all day. Hauled the old lady to her meeting, the girls out to the polo field, back to pick her up and back to the field." He sat at the table and took a long swallow from the can. "Waited till the game was over and squeezed out of that mess of traffic to get them into town to where they're having dinner. Gotta pick them up at ten."

"Did you see any of the game?" Paula asked as she set leftover meat loaf in the microwave oven and set the timer.

"Wouldn't waste my time. Bunch of horses with bandages on their legs, all getting in each other's way. Guys in fancy helmets whacking at a ball."

"All for sweet charity, Lew! Lots of money," Paula said. "Anyway, it's a game. For fun. Like a rodeo."

"Rodeo's a hell of a lot more than fun. It's...well, how to rope a calf, break a horse. Teaching people how to do things, not just showing off."

Paula grinned. "Seems I often saw you showing off. Remember that rodeo where you—"

He gave a satisfied smile. "Yeah, I was good, huh? Expert at that stuff."

"Sure, sure. I remember," Paula said, as she fashioned cold mashed potatoes into cakes, sprinkled paprika and set them sizzling in a frying pan. "But I'll have you know that these polo players are considered experts, too."

"Humph!" Lew unfolded the newspaper.

Paula turned the potato cakes, set muffins to warm in the oven. "Some are quite famous, renowned for their expertise all over the world."

Lew shrugged.

She removed the soda can, set out silver and napkins and bent to whisper in his ear. "Wanta hear a secret?" At his wary look, she gave him a conspiratorial wink and added, "I danced with the *most* famous one of all last night."

Lew's head jerked up. "You're joking."

She chuckled. It did seem like a joke. "The one they call the polo prince. He's very rich, very famous and *very* handsome. And I danced with him. I really did."

"You're joking," Lew said again, staring at her as she set out salads and filled two glasses with iced tea. "At least I hope to hell you are."

"No, I am not joking. It was so funny. I was working for Harry at the Moodys' costume ball, like I told you, remember? Well, I was in the pantry arranging canapés, and this man came in. I knew him immediately, in spite of his mask. Lord, I've heard him described a million times and I had seen his picture. Anyway, I was kinda dancing, like I do sometimes, and he..." She related the episode as she finished the dinner preparations. "He's a real good dancer, and...oh, golly, I hadn't danced in so long.... I guess I got carried away. I didn't realize we were actually in the ballroom until—"

"My God! Mrs. Ashford...she's gonna skin you alive."

"Don't be silly. Nobody saw me."

"Hang on a minute—you were in the ballroom, dancing with the big shot every gal in creation's got her eyes on, and you think nobody— Paula! Everybody saw you!"

"They didn't know who I was. I told you. He put a mask on me," she said, placing their filled plates on the table. "When some guy yelled 'Masks off' I hotfooted it out of there."

"You're crazy. How could they miss you? You didn't have on a costume."

"Oh, yes, I did. You should have heard Whitney and Rae this morning, trying to figure out who came dressed as a maid!" Paula almost choked on her iced tea. Now that the danger was past, it seemed very funny.

Lew wasn't laughing. "That was a damn fool thing to do."

"Oh, stop glaring at me like that. Nothing happened. The only thing is…" She touched her bare throat. "I lost my necklace, the one you gave me for my birthday. Remember, with the little gold horseshoe? I looked for it afterward, but—"

"You gonna lose more than that, fooling around with them high-society muck-a-mucks. Of all the damn fool shenanigans! Don't you know the old lady don't like nobody outshining her gals? And I don't like you messing around with them empty-headed, do-nothing, high-society folks."

"Oh, for goodness sake! I wasn't outshining anybody, and I certainly have no desire to associate with the likes of Whitney Ashford even if, heaven forbid, I should ever have the chance to do so."

"Well, seems to me you're all gaga about messing around with that pretty polo fellow."

"I wasn't messing around with him!"

"I'd like to know what you call it."

"An incident. One dance. Done. Over and out!" She spread her hands in a gesture of finality.

But there was a dreamy smile on her lips as she cleared the table and stacked the dishes. She was unaware that Lew watched her with anxious eyes.

The Green Acres polo field was a colorful sight as the players rode in and lined up for the first game of the Classic. But Brad Vandercamp was not looking at the field.

"Which is the Moodys' box?" he asked his friend Carl.

Carl pointed it out.

Brad started to move toward it, checked. He turned to Carl. "What's the daughter's name?"

Carl gazed thoughtfully at him. "Sheila. But that's not a good idea."

"Oh?"

"When the well-padded Brad Vandercamp glances in her direction, a lady gets ideas."

"Cut it out, Carl! Simple courtesy. Thank you for the ball, and—"

"Uh-huh. And, yes, thank you for the dinner invitation. I'm itching to come and meet that fascinating maid of yours, and oh, yes, by the way, return this thingamabob that she dropped when she danced with me at your ball. Damn it, Brad! You want to lose the woman her job?"

"Nothing so crude as that. I just want to—"

"I know what you want. And you'd do better to hang around the house somewhere near the servants' entrance."

"Like a stage-door johnny! Not on your life."

"Okay, okay. Do it your own way, chum. But..." Again Carl squinted thoughtfully. "What's the big deal? One dance. Why are you so hell-bent to find her?"

Brad shrugged but didn't answer. He didn't know why.

He fingered the necklace in his pocket and wondered. Why did he feel that if he let the woman with the saucy smile slip out of his life, he would lose something precious?

It was crazy, but there it was. He moved toward the Moody box and didn't hear Carl's last admonition. "Careful, buddy! Women get ideas even when you don't glance their way!"

CHAPTER THREE

THE Ashfords arose late the Sunday after the game. After all, it had been an exhausting week, with one social gathering after another. It was raining steadily and was a little chilly outside but warm and cozy in the cheerful breakfast room. The ladies lingered long over the delicious brunch Paula had prepared.

Sunday was officially Paula's day off. But if she had nowhere to go, which was often the case, the Ashfords considered her at their disposal. Even if she retreated to her uncle's quarters over the garage, she was easily on call. This morning she didn't mind. She wanted to hear about the game. She had never seen one, and knew nothing about polo. But she knew horses. It must take exceptionally skilled horsemanship to play a game in which horses were engaged. Her ears were alert as she replenished the basket of hot homemade rolls and poured cup after cup of coffee. But it was as if they had not seen the game. The conversation centered on who sat with whom in which spectator's box and who danced with whom when they retreated to the clubhouse.

"I don't think he saw me," Whitney complained. "Aunt Sally's box is in that far corner, next to the

Goosbys, who have all those guests. They blocked us off completely. We shouldn't have sat there."

Her mother sniffed. "And just where would you have us sit, missy! Nobody offered to share their box but my dear cousin. You should be grateful."

"But it is so disappointing that he never found where I was sitting."

"He found where Sheila Moody was sitting," Rae interjected.

Whitney stiffened. "That was her doing! She was smiling and simpering and hanging onto him like glue!"

Rae giggled. "I guess your view wasn't blocked by the Goosbys. You were watching them every minute."

"I was not! I only—"

"Girls, girls!" Mamie Ashford intervened.

"Well, I don't see why she's so het up about Brad Vandercamp," Rae said. "He's not the only interesting man who's here."

"He's the *most* interesting! And you needn't be so smug because his friend, Lord Carl Wormsley, earl of something or other, danced with you three times. He might have a title, but anything else he has is in hock!"

"I suppose you have checked the financial records of all the potential—"

"Word gets around!" Whitney snapped. "Rumor has it that his title is up for sale to the highest bidder, and I'm afraid that lets you out!"

Paula stopped listening. All she was hearing was that Whitney was in a snit. A few days later, she was in more of a snit. The prince had paid a call upon Sheila Moody.

Mrs. Ashford had heard of it at the bridge table. "One visit," she exclaimed. "And Ada Moody is hinting at a romance. I bet she's already looking at bridal clothes."

However, it seemed that the romance quickly cooled, and Whitney was somewhat mollified when the Ashfords received an invitation for a sojourn on *Renegade,* the Vandercamp yacht. They would be among the many guests who would dine and dance during a moonlight sail down the coast.

Paula received an invitation, too. Harry was catering, and he pleaded with her. To no avail. She couldn't take the risk.

What risk? He had probably forgotten all about her if he thought of her at all, and she...

All right. She was as anxious to view his yacht as she was to see him play polo.

Wrong. You're anxious to see him, idiot!

Well...out of sight, out of mind. She gave Harry a definite no.

Well, not exactly definite. When Harry persisted, she hesitated.

She'd never been on a sailboat, much less a yacht. And, from what she'd heard, the Vandercamp yacht was something to be seen.

Why not? With so many guests, he'd hardly notice one serving maid. Especially if she kept well out of his sight.

He recognized her the minute she stepped on the gangplank. He handed the binoculars to his steward, who stood beside him on the upper deck, and pointed. "That is she."

The steward nodded and hurried away.

Brad focused the binoculars on Paula. Caught by the buoyant enthusiasm reflected in her face, he felt his pulse quicken. That was why he had searched. For another glimpse of that face. Bright, smiling, bubbling with expectant wonder, as if always on the verge of some happy, exciting adventure.

Paula's eyes were wide as she ran up the gangplank. This wasn't a yacht, it was a ship! She tried to take it all in as she followed Harry and other workers across a deck that had been scrubbed and polished to a shining perfection. Down a hall and several spiral staircases to an oversize kitchen. No. It was called a galley, and it was equipped with ovens, refrigerators, counters and other appurtenances adequate for the average hotel. Certainly enough to accommodate one—

"Paula, honey, give me a hand here," Ruth, Harry's chief assistant, called. "These better go in the fridge. This here's some boat, ain't it?"

"Sure is." Paula lifted a carton of shrimp. "Guess he likes to travel in style."

"Shoot, he don't travel on it. Least he didn't coming here."

"Oh?" Paula tried to remember. The Ashfords had been so excited when the yacht—

"Guess it don't travel fast enough for him. He flew in from France or Italy...some fancy place on the Riviera where he was playing whatever game he plays there."

"So why the yacht?"

Ruth shrugged. "Who knows?" Guess no San Diego hotel is grand enough for him. Anyway, this boat, the *Renegade,* sailed in while he was still frolicking in Italy, and he's living abroad while here. Pretty decent living quarters, wouldn't you say?"

"Nice."

"One thing about working with Harry," Ruth said. "You get to know how the other half lives."

Right, Paula thought. At least Ruth certainly knew more about the prince than Whitney did. *Heck, I'm learning more than Whitney while fixing shrimp,* she thought, as Ruth rattled on.

"Costs a pretty penny just to park it—more than two thousand a day for a big one like this—and don't forget the crew that's always on hand, whether anybody's aboard or not...eight or ten I heard."

"That many?" Paula asked, incredulous.

"Oh, sure. Who's gonna maintain and sail the ship? There are those who maintain and sail this thing, as well as those who serve His Highness and guests who don't know how to pick up a plate for themselves."

"And all for one person."

"Oh, I don't think he's alone much, honey. I hear he's always got some special lady aboard."

"Oh?" Something else Whitney had missed. Was a lady—

"No lady with him now," Ruth said, answering the question Paula had not asked. "Some Italian woman back where he come from, but I guess he left her there. Seems like he gets bored pretty quick."

Paula remembered the mischievous eyes, the engaging smile. He hadn't looked bored. But maybe that was the way it began, and then... She felt her face grow hot and shook her head in irritation. As if something had begun the night of the costume ball! Good Lord! She was as foolish as Whitney. One impromptu dance and—

"And 'course there's always lots of entertaining, like this," Ruth went on.

"Plenty of bedrooms for overnight cruises. And we didn't have to supply no linen or china, stuff like that. And, Lord, if you'd seen the wine racks. I never—" She broke off at the appearance of a man, immaculate in a white tuxedo.

Harry turned from one of the ovens to greet him. "This is Mr. McCoy," he said, addressing his employees. "He is chief steward on the *Renegade,* and we are pleased to be working with him and his staff tonight. Now, as to procedure, as you know, bars and buffets are being set up on the two decks and at various indoor parlors. Each of you will now be assigned to certain sections where you will be assisted by one or more members of the regular *Renegade* staff.''

After a short conference between the two men, assignments and directions were made. Paula, who had received no assignment, assumed that she was to remain in the kitchen arranging the platters and hot dishes that would go up on dummy waiters to the various levels. But when Mr. McCoy arose from the table, he nodded to her. "Please, will you come with me?"

Puzzled, she followed him from the galley and up more and more staircases. After what seemed like an endless climb, they reached a landing, which he crossed to a door. He unlocked it with a card key and stepped back for her to enter.

She walked in, looked around. Commodious, but definitely a private parlor, she thought, noting a small table set for two.

She was to serve only two people? She turned to question the steward, but he inclined his head and quickly withdrew, closing the door behind him.

She looked at the table, the ice bucket with champagne beside it, a loaded buffet within easy reach. Serving only two would be a piece of cake. Since they weren't dining with the other guests, they obviously wanted to be alone. After serving them, she supposed she should, like Mr. McCoy, quietly withdraw. She chuckled. The only difficulty might be in finding her way to the galley.

Meanwhile, what had Ruth said? Yep, this was a good chance to see how the other half lives.

The sofa curving around the conversational area in one corner of the room was cushioned in shades of blue, somehow reminiscent of the tossing waves of the sea. The table centering the area held a big bowl of chrysanthemums that seemed to catch their color from the sunlit coastline displayed in the oversize picture on the wall. Everything spoke of good taste and money. She spotted a door, which she opened to a bedroom also tastefully done in shades of ocean blue.

Just as she started in, she felt the roll of the boat beneath her feet. They were off! Whoever she was to serve might come in at any moment, and she didn't want to be caught peeking. She quickly shut the door.

Just in time, she thought, as she heard the click of the card key and saw the other door open. She was standing at attention when he came in.

The prince himself.

Of course. Who else? Why hadn't it occurred to her before? Anybody who would sneak a servant he didn't even know on to a dance floor where she should not be would think nothing of sneaking away from his own guests to have a private rendezvous with…how had Ruth put it? His present interest.

She was surprised at her own indignation. Why should she care what he did, when and with whom?

Curiosity got the best of her, and she looked beyond him. Where was she?

"Hello, again," he said.

Her gaze flew to him. She had been too immersed in speculation to remember that he might recognize her.

She played it straight. "Good evening, sir. May I get you something? A drink or—"

"Allow me." He took the champagne from the ice bucket, uncorked it with practiced dexterity and poured two glasses. He handed one to her, touched it with his own. "To us."

What was going on? She set the glass down. "Thank you, sir, but I don't drink while working."

"You are not working. Tonight you are my guest."

"I—I... Beg pardon?" What kind of game was this?

"I said tonight you are my guest. So, please..." He pulled out a chair and smiled.

She did not move.

"Come now," he coaxed. "I've gone to a deal of trouble to arrange this bit of time. Let's relax and enjoy."

She saw the mischief lurking in his eyes. Remembered all she had heard of him.

She didn't like this arrangement. Didn't like being alone with a well-known lover boy, somewhere out in the Pacific, in his private quarters at the top of his yacht, locked...

Locked? Her throat felt dry. She moved to the door. It swung easily open, and she felt a flush of shame.

"You're not going to run away again, are you, Cinderella?" he asked, laughing.

Anger replaced the shame. "My name is not Cinderella."

"Oh? But you did run away at the stroke of midnight. Deserted—"

She was halfway out the door, but he blocked her way. "Wait. Don't go. Why are you so angry?"

"I'm not angry. I just—" She bit back the words *don't intend to be one of your easy pickups.* "I don't indulge in fairy-tale games, Mr. Vandercamp."

"This isn't a game."

"Whatever you call it, I don't like it. I came here to work, and I find myself tricked into...into this!" Her gesture expressed what she couldn't bring herself to say.

"What's wrong with *this*? How else was I to find you?"

"What?"

"No name. No place of residence. I didn't even know where you worked. Naturally I assumed you were in the employ of the Moodys, and made several calls there. Saw no trace of you. It was only by lucky chance that during one of these visits, Sam, Moody's son, dropped a hint. The costume ball was served by an outfit called Harry's Catering Service. So—''

Paula, who had been fascinated into silence as much by his clipped British accent as his rapid words, broke in. "So why didn't you just ask Harry? That would have been simple."

"You think so? Of course I considered that avenue. But it seems Mr. Harry is reluctant to release information concerning his employees, ostensibly for their protection but, I surmise, more for his own. According to my father, one hates to have key personnel stolen from one."

"Oh."

"And what could I say? Blond hair...no, more gold than blond. Laughing blue eyes. About five foot four, with a just-right figure. Great dancer...light as a feather in my arms." His mouth twitched. "Such a description might have a certain...well, unsavory connotation. I would not like to create such an impression. You do understand?"

"Of course." In spite of herself, her lips curved in accord with his infectious grin.

"Likewise, the idea of a detective was abhorrent to me. As if I were in pursuit of a criminal or had some devious intent."

"Yes, that would be rather tacky," she said, entering into the game.

"Right. So you see why there's a party aboard the *Renegade* tonight. And why it's being catered by...guess who?"

She stared at him. "All that trouble. All these people. Why?"

"I just told you. I was having the devil of a time. I didn't know your name. Still don't, incidentally. Nor—"

"No. I mean why did you want to find me?"

The question seemed to puzzle him. He hesitated, smiled. "We do dance well together, don't we?"

"That's no reason."

"It's a beginning. There may be other things we do well together. Wouldn't you like to find out?"

Again she saw the mischief in his eyes. "I...I don't think—"

"Oh, don't be so wary. I am a gentleman. And," he added quickly as if he just remembered, "there was another reason I had to find you. I had something of yours that I was anxious to return to you. See?" He reached into his pocket and held it out to her.

"My necklace! You found it." She was genuinely pleased.

"Actually, you left it with me when you withdrew. The chain snapped and—"

"And you had it fixed. No, replaced it," she corrected, examining the new chain, a little heavier and obviously more expensive. Some basic rule about accepting expensive jewelry from a man... Maybe she ought not to accept. But she was so pleased to have it back. She looked at him, her face glowing. "Thank you. It's very special to me."

He touched the small charm. "You like horses?"

"Oh, yes!"

"I knew it! A lady after my own heart." He took her arm and ushered her to the table. "Sit down. Let's eat, drink and be merry while finding what else we have in common."

"I'm sorry, Mr. Vandercamp. I do appreciate what you've done, but—"

He picked up her glass and handed it to her. "My name's Brad. What's yours?"

CHAPTER FOUR

"YOU'VE hardly touched this," he said later, as he removed their salad plates. "Aren't you hungry?"

"Oh. Yes, I am, only I feel..." Unreal, like she was floating on some imaginary cloud. But this was real. And it wasn't true that he didn't know how to pick up a plate. *He's waiting on me! Deftly, with the same casual ease with which he opened the champagne,* she thought as he set a filled plate before her.

She tried to smile. "I'm not used to being waited on."

"Enjoy. Tonight, I am here to grant your every wish, my fair lady."

The savory scent of Harry's famous Maiale al Pepe drifted from the plate. She looked at the succulent circles of pork in the tasty herb sauce, the tiny, crisp, not overdone string beans, rice with its separate grains still steaming. Amazing. Sent all the way from the galley and kept piping hot on—

He looked at her from across the table. "Now what are you thinking?"

About how the other half lives, she thought. "That this is very delicious," she said.

"Then bon appetit!" He lifted his wineglass.

She touched it with hers, trying to relax.

"And stop looking as if you're about to pull that Cinderella act again!"

"What?"

"As if you might run out on me any minute."

"I...I do feel a little awkward," she said honestly. "It's like... Well, you have run out on your guests, and—"

"I did no such thing. I welcomed each one as they came aboard."

"But now you're here, and they—"

"Are eating and drinking, just as you and I. The decks, dance hall and private parlors are at their disposal. They won't miss me."

"But you..." She stopped, taken aback by the revelation. He really didn't know that he was the main attraction.

"Well?" he prompted. "You were saying?"

"That you should be with your friends. It doesn't seem right for us to be hiding away up here while your party goes on below."

"But I'm trying to make a new friend." He smiled, and she was caught by the way his eyes laughed as if at some mysterious joke. "That's the whole point. I wanted us to have this time to ourselves so we could really get acquainted and..." He paused, his fork halfway to his mouth, and frowned. "Hiding? Oh, I hadn't thought... You'd prefer us to be more public?"

"No! I didn't mean—"

"Well, why not! I hired the same band that the Moodys had. Let's go down and dance!"

"Oh, sure." She touched her uniform. "I'm dressed for it."

"No problem," he said. "My mother's about your size and keeps a wardrobe aboard. Dozens of formals. After we eat, I'll go down and fetch one for you." He seemed delighted by the idea.

She gasped. "Do you want me to lose both my jobs?"

"Oh. I see. You think Mr. Harry wouldn't like…" He stared at her. "Both? You've got two jobs?"

"Yes. I also work for Mrs. Ashford. She and her daughters are here tonight, and they…" *Would have a howling conniption if I walked in on the arm of the prize catch of the year,* she thought. "Would not like it if I were to appear among the guests," she said.

"I see. Just as well," he said. "I like having you all to myself. Only…why do you have two jobs?"

"Some of us must earn our way," she blurted. And wanted to bite her tongue! That was a nasty crack to someone who didn't have to earn his way.

He didn't get it. "Doesn't leave much time for riding," he said.

"Riding?"

He gestured toward the horseshoe charm, now lying against her throat. "You said you like horses."

"Oh. I do. But they're a long way off, anyway."

"Your horses?"

"Not mine. Except one," she added, and smiled, suddenly deep in memory. "Spitfire. That's what we called her, because that's what she was, and that's why Dad could buy her. Jake, the trader, was about ready to give her away, she was so wild and almost untrainable. But my dad's real good with horses. He broke her in and gave her to me that Christmas. She's still spirited and...well, quite a horse."

"You miss her, don't you?"

"Yes. I do miss her, and I miss..." Mom. Dad. The rolling hills of the ranch. "I guess I miss being there."

"Where is there?"

"Wyoming. The Randolph ranch. My dad's one of the ranch hands."

"And you lived there?"

"All of my life till now."

"And you liked it."

"Oh, yes. We had our own house, because Mom was the family cook. I loved it. There was a creek to swim in, a cave and horses. It was a fun place to grow up in."

He looked at her glowing face. This was the woman who danced while she worked. "No," he said. "It's not the place. It's you."

"What do you mean?"

"You seem to have fun wherever, or whatever you're doing. Tell me. If you like the ranch so much, why are you here?"

She hesitated, smiled. "Oh, it's an idea I have, but it's a long way off and very complicated. Anyway, that's enough about me. I'd rather hear about you."

"All right. Fair enough." He scratched his nose. "Let's see. I grew up in the county of Surrey in my mother's old home, Balmour. I—"

"I don't mean all that tabloid stuff. I want to know about the real you, what you do and what you like." She laughed. "Oh, I guess that's in the tabloids, too. You like polo, and you're really good at it, and that's why they call you the polo prince."

"I'm not all that good. The guys dubbed me prince when I was at Sandhurst. I was the only guy on the team without a real title. It was a kind of joke."

"Do you mind?"

"The joke?"

"No. Not having a title."

"Lord, no! Back home, titles are as common as shillings...well, guineas, anyway." He chuckled. "Guineas, on the other hand, are a deal harder to come by."

He looked as if he didn't care about either the titles or the guineas, she thought. "Anyway, you must be good at polo, to play at all," she said. "It sounds pretty complicated to me."

"You've never seen a game?"

"No."

"Well, we'd better take care of that. We're playing Tuesday, and I'll get space for you in—"

"No, don't! I...might not be able to make it. Maybe you'd better just tell me about the game... how you manage with those horses."

"Later." He didn't want to talk about polo. "Come, let's have our coffee on the deck."

"Oh, my goodness!" she exclaimed, as he slid a glass door open and stepped back. "How did I miss this?"

"What?"

"Your own private deck! I didn't see it, so busy snooping inside. I hope you don't mind." Before he could tell her that he didn't mind anything she did, she was across the deck and at the rail, gazing into the distance. The deck was on a point at the very front of the yacht where, when at sail, the wind was sharp. She didn't seem to notice that it whipped through her curls, snatched away the little lace cap. When he joined her, her voice came out in an awed whisper. "It's so...so incredibly beautiful."

He nodded, suddenly conscious of the late sunset. The great red-gold ball that was the sun was slowly sinking, its glow reflected in myriad colors, violet, yellow, blue, that seemed to blend sky and sea together. Had he ever noticed it before?

"Makes you feel good, doesn't it?" she asked. "Like you shouldn't worry about anything. Everything is going to be all right."

He smiled at her. "You get all of that out of one sunset?"

"It's like my dad says. As long as the sun goes down and the moon comes up, you know somebody up there is in charge and the world isn't really crazy."

"Your dad sounds like quite a philosopher."

"Guess so. He's always saying things like that." For a long time she was silent, seemingly absorbed, her eyes darting from the distant horizon to the churning waves. Finally she turned to him and sighed. "I should feel guilty."

"Why?"

"I should be down in the galley working my head off instead of..." She hesitated, shrugged. "Instead of standing here, happy as a lark, sailing into a golden wonderful horizon."

"Nonsense." He looked at her curls, dancing in the wind, her eyes bright with joy. He'd like to keep her that way. "You shouldn't feel guilty."

She gave a gurgle of laughter. "I don't. I told you. I'm happy as a lark. Do you know this is the first time I've gone sailing? Except with Toby, which surely doesn't count."

"Toby?"

"The foreman's son. We built a little raft, which we kept on the creek, and sometimes we'd pack a lunch and go sailing off to—"

"Wait." He took her hand, feeling suddenly possessive. "Maybe you'd better tell me more about

Toby...about your life on the ranch. Stay put," he said, seating her in one of the lounge chairs near a bolted table. "I'll bring coffee."

They sipped coffee, munched on fruit and cheese and talked.

He wanted to know about Toby.

"Toby? Oh, he was just a childhood friend," she said, surprised to find that Toby had become just that. A friend who had grown up, become a banker and married a girl name Cynthia. A friend who had become only a distant, unimportant memory.

"You said you went sailing with him."

"Oh." She told him. About the day the raft overturned and Toby got a walloping from his dad, who had told him not to go near the rapids. They could have been drowned.

"That was silly. We were both good swimmers, and the rapids weren't all that rapid. My mom was mad as fire at the way Mr. Jones lit into Toby. She said he wouldn't wallop his horse, and she didn't believe in walloping kids. Do you?" she asked, surprised how eager she was for his opinion.

He shook his head. "Maybe an occasional tap on the behind like my old nanny would give me when I—"

"You had a nanny?"

"Of course." He gave her a doesn't-everyone look. "Until I was almost five, and then there was a tutor, and then..."

All thoughts of her companions slaving below

faded from her mind as this man with the oh-so-English voice told her about himself. Little things... the way his nanny's teeth clicked when she told him that little men didn't cry, but Swen, one of the gardeners, said different. "It ain't unmanly to cry for someone you love." Swen had helped him bury Smokey, his spaniel, secretly in the family plot, because, "By gorry, Smokey's been more of a someone to you than anybody else. And saved your life, he did. If the snake hadn't got him, t'would surely been you!"

She smiled at his mimicry of the gardener's Scottish accent and felt sorry for a lonely boy about whom only a gardener cared.

It seemed no time at all before the sunlight faded into darkness, and she was at the rail again, this time gazing at the stars. "Starlight, star bright, first star I see tonight. I wish I may, I wish I might, have the wish I wish tonight," she quoted.

"And what do you wish tonight?"

"I can't. The first star you see is the one you wish on, and I missed it, I was so busy talking."

"I'm sorry."

"Don't be. I must have made a hundred wishes on a hundred first stars. And I..." *Wouldn't have missed our talk for all the world,* she thought. "I think I like seeing them all at once like this. Aren't they spectacular? I'm glad there's no moon."

"It's getting cool. You'd better have this," he

said, taking off his jacket and draping it over her shoulders.

It was warm from his body and carried the fresh scent of his aftershave. *It's like being wrapped in a bit of him,* she thought, giddy with pure sensual pleasure.

"Why are you glad there's no moon?"

"Oh, I, er…" *This is what it means to be tongue-tied,* she thought. *It's just his jacket, stupid.*

"What do you have against the moon?"

"Nothing," she said, managing to get control of her voice. "But haven't you heard? The blacker the night, the brighter the stars."

"No, I don't believe I have."

"Well, it's true. Moonlight tends to block off the stars to some extent. But on a black night like this, the stars have a ball, and shine in all their glory. So clear. See? You can even tell which stars twinkle and which are still."

"Is that true? Some twinkle and some don't?"

She gave him an exasperated look. "Haven't you ever looked at the stars?"

He smiled, glanced up, then at her. "Well, now that you mention it, perhaps not…not really."

"Well, look. See that one right there?" She pointed. "See how it twinkles. And the one next to it is so still." She began to point and answer his questions. "I don't know why some twinkle and some don't. Dad says it probably has something to do with movement." She pointed out the Big

Dipper. "The Big Dipper moves, you know. I used to watch it every night when I was home, to see which way it tilted. But no matter which way, the two stars on the front of the cup always point to the North Star. See? That's how sailors could tell which way was north long before a compass was heard of."

"How do you know so much about the stars?" he asked.

"My dad. He liked to study them. Especially when he was out on the range. Always took his binoculars with him. Said it got lonesome out there at night, and the stars kept him company."

"That's a strange concept."

"Yes, isn't it? But that's my dad. He says sure as shooting there was some lonesome cowboy on one of those stars gazing this way, just as Dad was looking toward him."

"So he believes there are human beings on other planets?"

"Definitely. Says we'll soon find out if we keep flying around in space. As he puts it, we'd be plumb loco to think somebody up there made this whole universe just for the likes of us!" She laughed, expecting him to join in.

He didn't. "I'd like to meet your dad," he said.

"Well... Yes." Not very likely, she thought. "Did your mom or dad talk to you about the stars?" she asked, curious. He hadn't mentioned either of them.

He looked surprised. "No. We didn't do much talking. Guess we were all too involved."

"Even when you were little?"

"Oh, sure. Seems there is always something going on...a charity ball, hunt or house party either at our place or elsewhere. And they travel a good deal. My father's quite an entrepreneur, business all over the world."

"And you?"

"Pardon?"

"What do you do?"

"Lots of things. Tennis, golf, not to mention polo. And I travel quite a bit myself."

"Oh." Again she wanted to bite her tongue, because that wasn't at all what she meant.

Never mind. Again, he didn't get it. What else did one do, but play?

And what's wrong with that? Would you work if you didn't have to?

She supposed not. But wouldn't she feel useless and a little bored if all she did was—

"What do you like to do?"

"Swim. And I'm fairly good at tennis," she answered quickly. She wasn't about to pull another boner. "And..." She looked at him. "I must tell you. I very much enjoyed...this." *You. Just talking to you,* she thought, but her gesture took in the yacht, the ocean, sailing. "Thank you."

"Thank *you*," he said, but his eyes said more.

She wasn't sure why what happened next happened. Maybe it was in the eyes.... The loneliness of a child who had only a gardener to talk to. The mischief of a man who knew how to play...and listen...and laugh.

She didn't know why. She just knew she had to touch him.

She reached a hand to caress his cheek, lifted her lips for a light kiss.

Only... Her lips seemed to cling, and she couldn't let go. He pulled her close and deepened the kiss, sending delightful, exhilarating sensations vibrating through her. She wound her arms tightly around his neck, wanting the feeling to last forever.

Time seemed to stop, and she was aware of nothing but the man who held her, tracing light kisses along her face, ruffling her hair and murmuring endearments. Then, as if from a great distance, she heard the hoot of a passing steamer, reminding her...bringing her out of the trance.

She tried to pull away.

He held on. "Don't run away from me, my little Cinderella."

Cinderella! That did it. Gave her the strength to break away. "I...I'm sorry. I have to..." *Get the soiled linens and dishes on the dummy waiter,* she thought. *Get down to the galley where I'm supposed to be before somebody comes looking for me.*

She tried to smile. "Time to go to work," she called as she rushed inside.

CHAPTER FIVE

"You did what!" Lew shouted. "Have you gone bananas?"

"Oh, for goodness sake, *I* didn't *do* anything," she said, tossing dirty socks in the pile she would launder. "Honestly, Lew, how you can make such a mess in just one week is beyond me."

"Nobody asked you to clean it up. And we're not talking about me. We're talking about the mess you're making with your life!"

"What do you mean? My life is just fine. I—"

"Don't pull that innocent act on me. I know you, Paula. You're so spaced out with that—"

"I am not!"

"Don't tell me. I know that look."

"What look?"

"That stars popping out of your eyes got the world on a string look. Like a ride on some fancy boat was the greatest thing that ever happened to you."

"It wasn't the boat. It was..." She chuckled. "Maybe it was the world. You sure get a different view of it from up there." That golden sun sinking into the ocean. The unblocked expanse of moon and stars, the—

"Damn right, it wasn't the boat. I seen that same look the other night, when you was swishing around the kitchen talking about dancing like a fool at that costume to-do."

"Come on. That was just a...kind of joke."

"More'n a joke, girl. I seen it in your eyes. All bright and excited like they were the Christmas your pa give you that mare."

"Spitfire?" How did her horse get into this? And why was Lew so mad?

"Yeah, Spitfire. You looked at her like you were the luckiest girl in the world! Excited, ready to take off to heaven on that feisty mare that was about as tame as a galloping tornado. I tried to tell your pa she was too damn dangerous for you to handle."

"I did handle her. I only took one tumble."

"It was a big one. And let me tell you..." Lew stood and pointed a finger at her. "It's nothing to the tumble you'll take if you keep fooling around with that prince fellow!"

"Oh, for goodness sake!" Paula turned from him and tossed empty beer bottles and other trash into a wastebasket. "I am not fooling around with him!" she said, polishing the counter with a burst of energy.

"No? I'd like to know what you call sneaking up to—"

"I did not sneak! I was taken up there. To work, I thought. He..." She stopped, not wanting to sound like she had been tricked into something.

"Oh, yeah! He fixed it, did he? Fixed it so he could be all cozy-cozy with... By golly, Paula, if he took advantage of you, I'll... Did he? Tell me, Paula, did he touch you?"

"No, he didn't!" Not until she... But she could no more have stopped herself from touching him than she could have stopped breathing.

"By golly, if he did! If he tried any funny stuff with you, I'll—"

"I told you he didn't!" He could have. In his arms, his lips against hers, she was so giddy with longing that... "It wasn't like—like you think. It was..." Compelling, sweet and intimate.

"Taking his time, huh?"

"What?" She stared at him in some confusion.

"I know what he's up to."

"He's not up to anything!" Suddenly she was angry. She turned to face him. "I told you he was— *is* a perfect gentleman."

"Look, girl, you don't tell me what he is. I've been around a hell of a lot more than you. Ain't got your book learning, but I got street smarts. I know about rich playboys, Paula. They got a line a mile long, and it's baited with money, ready to reel in some innocent like you."

"He didn't have any kind of line. We just talked."

"You wouldn't know a line if you heard it. That's how they do...come on all proper, butter up a girl.

Till they get tired and dump her like she's trash. By golly, the next time he gets near you, I'll—"

"Oh, for goodness sake, when would he ever get near me again! There won't be a next time."

"Well, there'd better not be," he muttered. He seemed mollified, but still looked anxious. He stood at the bedroom door and watched her rip the sheets off his bed. "You don't need to change them sheets every week, Paula. Shoot, when I was in the bunkhouse, sometimes I didn't—"

"This isn't the bunkhouse, and I won't have my uncle living in a pigsty."

For the most part, he was silent as she finished cleaning. But as she started to leave he took her hand. "You're a sweet girl, Paula."

She wrinkled her nose. "I know."

"Too damn sweet. I'm sorry I yelled at you. Lord knows, you get enough of that from Mrs. High and Mighty."

"Oh, she's not so bad. It's just that she's usually not feeling so well."

"Yeah. Drunk as a skunk. Anyway, I'm sorry I yelled at you. But for all your book smarts, you're pretty dumb about...well, about the facts of life. I worry about you." He ran a hand through his hair. "And, well, I did promise your pa I'd look after you."

"I know." She stood on tiptoe to kiss him. "So look after me. And yell all you please."

"But do you listen?"

"Yes. I really do. So you needn't worry. Take those down, will you?" she asked, pointing to two overflowing wastebaskets. She kissed him again, picked up the bundle to be laundered and went out.

He's such a worrywart, she thought as she made her way downstairs. *I should never have told him.*

Why had she?

Habit. Hadn't she always confided in Lew? At least when he lived at the ranch and seemed to be as much a child as she and Toby. He had helped them build that ill-fated raft. He knew about their plans to marry and buy a ranch when they grew up, and how she was going to be a veterinarian. It was Lew, who had probably never read a book in his life, who brought her all the James Herriot books, which she devoured over and over again. How many cold winter nights had she sat by a cozy fire and trudged with that well-known vet through snow-filled English hills to save a sick sheep or deliver a calf that was turned the wrong way? That was what she was going to do when she grew up!

She smiled. Childhood dreams. And she had shared them all with Lew.

Habit. It had seemed natural to tell him about the boat ride. Anyway, she had nobody else to talk to, and she was bursting to tell someone. She dare not even tell Ruth, who had been sweating in the galley while she was living it up like a grand lady.

She chuckled as she shifted her bundle and opened the back door. Now that it was over, it did seem like a grand but definitely secret adventure. A different and, yes, really delightful experience.

And...well, funny, the way it happened.

No. The way he *made* it happen, she thought as she entered the laundry room and began to sort the clothes. Just to find her. He had visited the Moodys, traced her to Harry's and... Had he really gone to all that trouble, arranged that whole party aboard his yacht, invited all those people just to get to see her?

He said so.

You're an idiot if you believe that, Paula Grant. That was just a line he was giving you to...

A line? Now, for goodness sake, she was thinking like Lew. So suspicious.

Weren't you?

Maybe a little...at first.

Maybe nothing! She giggled as she threw in the white things and turned on the washer. Lord, the way she had bolted to that door!

And felt like a fool when she found it wasn't locked.

Nobody forced her to stay there. She could have left.

And done what? Gone to the galley and made some excuse about being sent to the wrong place? Or found she wasn't needed or something? She sure couldn't have told the truth. That would have sounded a good deal like harassment or something.

It wasn't like that at all.

And you wanted to stay, didn't you? She leaned on the washer and watched the water flow in.

She had leaned against a rail, waves gushing far below, wind whistling through her hair, sun on her face. A man standing beside her.

He hadn't seemed like a rich playboy with a line. Just an ordinary... No, she couldn't call him ordinary. There was something about him that she couldn't quite define, something that made him... special?

No, she couldn't say that, either. He was...well, just fun to be with.

And he hadn't made a pass or anything like that. He didn't even try to hold on to her when she finally came to her senses and broke away. He had just laughed and followed her in and...and actually helped her!

She chuckled, remembering how together they had dumped all the dishes and silver onto the dummy, rolled up the soiled linens and made the place spotless. Just as if they were in this together. Two truants who had stolen time off from work for just a little fun.

When they finished, he had been reluctant for her to leave. "Don't leave. We're not even back to shore. The party isn't over yet."

"It is for Cinderella," she said, knowing the galley was a madhouse with all the cleaning, storing and packing up. "This was...." She hesitated, not quite sure how to put it. "Fun. It was all wrong, and

I shouldn't have enjoyed it. But I did,'' she said, with her usual blatant honesty. ''Thank you, and goodbye.''

This time she was out the door before he could stop her. She did find her way to the galley and joined the gang just like she had been working all evening, and nobody suspected anything.

So where was the harm? The Polo Classic would end in a couple of days, and he would be on his merry way, and she would be...

Good heavens! The wash cycle was almost over, and she hadn't added the detergent and bleach! She dumped in both and started the cycle again, then hurried into the kitchen to start dinner.

She was intercepted by Rae. ''Paula, Mother says forget the chicken. Have Lew pick up the meat for the rack of lamb you do and whatever else you need to go with it. I just talked to Lord Wormsley on the phone, and he's coming to dinner and bringing a friend. And you know who's his best friend, don't you, Paula?'' Rae asked, her eyes wide.

Who else? Paula thought. The prince. Whitney would get her chance.

''So you'll have to mend this. See where I snagged it?'' Rae held up the strapless turquoise dress that was her favorite. ''I want to look my best. And Whitney says have Lew pick up her things from the cleaner's. Oh, yes, and Mother wants him to serve and be sure to wear that tux she bought him.

And she says for you to check his nails. She doesn't want him to look like he's the gardener."

Which is just one of his disguises, Paula thought, unable to restrain a chuckle as she thought of him in the role of butler. The proverbial bull in the china shop.

Rae pondered. "Let's see. What else? Flowers, she said you could arrange them from the garden. You do it so well. And candles. She set it at seven, and she wondered if you would have time to make your rolls."

Paula glanced at the kitchen clock. Three. She shook her head. "I'll pick up some at the bakery." She'd have to step on it to get everything ready on time. She hoped Lew's fancy shirt was clean.

She did finish in record time, table beautifully set, dinner ready and Lew stuffed into the tuxedo. It wasn't her fault that Lew spilled soup down Mrs. Ashford's back, knocked over Whitney's wineglass and the friend who was brought wasn't the prince.

The missing prince was the worst disaster. "Why didn't he bring him?" Whitney moaned. "It would have been only common courtesy. He's staying on his yacht, isn't he, and supposed to be his best friend! It's your fault, Rae. You should have insisted that he bring the prince! I'm sure he would have been anxious to—"

"Oh, I don't know about that," Rae said. For once, she was looking smug. "The prince has a way of eluding people, don't you think? Even at his own party on the yacht, he always seemed to be somewhere else. At least I never saw him, did you?"

Whitney ignored this pointed remark. "Such a shame. This would have been such an opportunity to be...well, more intimate. Oh, dear, only two more days, and he will be gone."

The two days swiftly passed. As Paula helped the Ashford women dress to go to the final game, she wished with all her heart that she could go with them. This was her last chance to see him play. To see him at all. She brushed that thought aside. It was just that she had never seen a polo game, she told herself.

Afterward, she did hear from the excited women that the English team won the Classic. But not much else, not even who sat with or talked to whom. The excited women were too busy primping for the grand victory ball. This would be their last chance to impress the prince.

He wasn't there. Paula heard that the next morning, as she served a late breakfast to the ladies.

"Can you imagine that?" Whitney chewed viciously on a piece of toast. "He didn't even have the common courtesy to attend. And he should have been the one to receive the trophy for his team instead of that pompous Lord Wormsley with all that gushing about being honored to be here for such a charitable endeavor and—"

"He did not gush!" Rae's cup clattered against her saucer. "And he certainly was not pompous! He said not one word about the excellence of his team. Just how honored they were to be here and participate in such a worthy cause, how proud we should be that we had raised so much for the children's home."

Paula, filling Whitney's cup, reflected that this was the first time she had heard the children's home mentioned. That was a worthy cause. She wondered how much they had raised.

"Well, he went on and on!" Whitney said. "I wanted him to shut up and tell us where the prince was."

"Didn't matter where, did it?" Rae's mouth twisted. "He wasn't at the ball. Wasn't gazing into your sensitive eyes!"

"Oh, shut up! You needn't be so smug. Nobody was gazing into your eyes, either. And your precious lord is gone. Along with the prince. The *Renegade* sailed out this morning. So there!" Whitney sniped at her sister. Her face was a mask of fury, frustration and defeat. "He's gone!"

Gone. The word echoed in Paula's ears, and something deep inside her went numb. She would never see him again. Never see his eyes fill with mischief, hear his voice, touch...

For goodness sake. She was being as foolish as Whitney!

She was glad Mrs. Ashford came in, crossly demanding that Paula do something about her poor head.

Paula rushed to attend her. It was good to be busy, she thought, It kept her from thinking.

But no matter how hard she worked, how busy she kept, the sad feeling didn't go away.

The name was on the mailbox. Ashford.

He drove past the house twice before he drove around the corner and parked.

He would go down the driveway to the service entrance. Shouldn't attract any notice in these old jeans and sweatshirt.

Lew didn't recognize designer jeans, but he recognized the prince immediately. He stood up from the flower bed he was weeding and eyed him suspiciously. "Good day, sir. Can I help you?"

"I hope so. I'm looking for a Miss Grant. Paula Grant."

"Sorry. This is the Ashford residence."

"I know. But I thought... I was under the impression that Miss Grant is employed here."

"Employed, yes. But she don't receive visitors."

"I...well, I suppose not. I understand." Why was this gardener being so bloody disagreeable? "This is not really a social visit. I just wanted to contact her. If you would be kind enough to inform her that—"

"Sorry. She's not here."

Damn. The man was giving him the runaround. Brad saw red. "Listen, my dear fellow, whoever you are, I simply wish to arrange to—"

"I ain't your dear fellow! And you ain't arranging a damn thing with her. Get it?"

Brad stared, more surprised than irritated. Perhaps this was Ashford himself. He certainly had not the demeanor of a servant. "I beg your pardon. I'd like to explain. I am—"

"I know who you are, and I'm not about to let Paula get mixed up with the likes of you."

For a moment Brad was speechless. Never in his life had he been so addressed, either by servant or peer. It threw him off. He swallowed, began again. "My dear sir—"

"Lew, I wanted you to—" Both men looked at Mrs. Ashford, who stood in the doorway. "Oh, my! I—we thought you were gone! I mean..." She stared at Brad. "Mr. Vandercamp! Brad. My dear boy, what are you doing... I mean how delightful to have you here," she babbled, obviously caught between confusion and awe.

"Good afternoon, Mrs. Ashford," Brad said. "I came to—"

"He asked for Miss Whitney." The impudent man broke in before Brad could utter another word. He glared at Brad, daring him to deny it.

"Oh, my, how perfectly wonderful. I mean, she'll be delighted. Do come in." She hesitated. "No, you shouldn't. Whatever are you doing back here? Lew, do show him around to the front." She blinked, or rather twinkled at him, Brad thought. "You must make a proper entrance on your first visit to my house," she said.

CHAPTER SIX

BRAD, thoroughly disgusted, followed the man, as puzzled as he was furious. Asked for Miss Whitney, indeed! He was about to ask what the hell prompted such a lie, but the man spoke first.

"This here job means a lot to Paula," he said.

This was no explanation. "I have no wish to jeopardize her job. I only—"

"And Mrs. Ashford don't like her having callers," the man continued as if he hadn't spoken.

"Then perhaps..." Brad stopped. *Better not leave a message with him. Whoever he is, it's obvious that he also objects to callers. Or to me! He doesn't even know me. And...a gardener? What gives him the right to object to anything?*

Before he could question his proprietary stance, the gardener's rapid strides had taken them to the front entrance.

A beaming Mrs. Ashford opened the door. "Come in, come in. This is such a delightful surprise. Whitney will be down in a moment, and..."

He followed her in, wondering what explanation he could give that wouldn't jeopardize Paula and wouldn't involve him with Whitney. He'd just been through that kind of mistake with Sheila Moody.

* * *

The visit had occurred on a Thursday, Paula's half-day off, and she had been at school that afternoon and evening. As it happened, the Ashford women left the house early the next morning and were out most of the day. So Paula did not hear of the prince's visit until the next evening as she served dinner.

Then she heard plenty. And Lew had said not one word! She could hardly wait for them to finish eating.

When they finally left the table, she stalked in from the dining room, set the pile of dirty dishes in the sink, placed her hands on hips and flashed an accusatory eye at her uncle. "So! You didn't tell me the prince himself was here yesterday!"

Lew's fork clattered to the floor, and he bent for it. When he surfaced, there was a deep flush on his cheeks. His mouth was open, but he couldn't seem to speak.

"Well, why didn't you?"

"Now, listen, Paula. You ain't got no cause to be mad just 'cause I didn't—"

"Mad? Why should I be mad?"

"Look." Lew put down his fork. "I didn't do nothing."

"Oh, yes, you did! You deliberately kept it from me, didn't you?"

"No, I—"

"As if I wouldn't get it all from in there!" Paula jerked her head toward the dining room. "That's all they talked about while I was serving dinner. In detail. How he first came to the back, so you knew—"

"I wanted to spare you, Paula."

He looked so wary that she couldn't help needling him. "Then you should have told me." She put a hand to her heart. "Should have spared me the pain, the humiliation of hearing from another that—" She broke off. He looked so upset, she stopped teasing him. "Hey, buck up! I'm just putting you on!" She put an arm around his shoulder. "But you must stop trying to protect me."

Lew pushed his plate aside. "It's just that I don't want you hurt. I—"

"Oh, for goodness sake! Did you think I'd really care that he came to see Whitney?"

Lew's eyes widened.

"You needn't look so surprised! I told you I am not, as you put it, spaced out about him. Why should I care whom he visits?"

"I...I didn't know," Lew muttered.

"Well, now you know. I'm not one bit jealous or hurt or anything stupid like that!" She swallowed the lump in her throat and gave him a bright smile. "So come on, finish your dinner," she said, putting his plate in front of him.

"Well..." He took up his fork but didn't look too relieved.

He's not convinced, she thought. Determined to reassure him, she adopted a lighthearted manner as she rinsed dishes and recounted what she had learned in the dining room. "Whitney is beside herself," she said, talking as rapidly as she worked. "All smug confidence again. Says she knew there was something between them from the first, and she doesn't believe, as he said, that he just happened by. On his way out, he said, to look at a ranch he's thinking of buying."

At this Lew looked up. "What the hell does he want with a ranch?"

"For his polo ponies. He likes playing at Green Acres but doesn't like his ponies crowded in with others at the club, so when his trainer mentioned this little ranch..."

"Why don't he just ship 'em back from wherever he come from?" Lew asked, sounding irritated.

"Oh, he's taken a fancy to this area and might stick around a bit." She chuckled. "Whitney says he's sticking around on account of *her*."

Lew grunted.

"Oh, yes, she says something clicked between them the minute he looked into her eyes and she knew it couldn't possibly be over. Says she had this strange feeling deep in her bones that when his yacht pulled out, he wasn't on it."

"Humph!"

"Well, she was right. He wasn't on it. Seems his mother desired to take a party on a cruise of the Caribbean. So the captain sailed the craft through the canal to the Florida coast, where she and her party will fly in from England. Just imagine," she said a little dreamily. "Ranches, yachts, any little thing you want. Just snap your fingers and it's there! Must be nice, huh?"

"Nice," her uncle said. "If things are what you got a mind for."

That's what's on her mind, Paula thought, remembering the greed in Whitney's eyes as she talked of her prospects.

Things. Brad had had things all his life. But no one to talk to.

She felt sad.

"Now what are you thinking?"

"Oh! Nothing. Well, about Whitney," she said quickly, seeing Lew's concerned look. She'd been talking too fast. He said whenever she talked like a house afire, sure as shooting, something was wrong. Goodness, nothing was wrong, and she didn't want him thinking it was!

"I was just thinking how excited she...they all were over one visit. They even served him tea, because they said that's what English people do at that time. Served it themselves, too, because I was gone and you were working in the yard." She chuckled. "Not that you'd have known what to fix any more than they did. I sure would've liked seeing them stirring around trying to fix anything. And Lord knows what they served beside my apricot tarts."

She stopped. Talking too fast again. She took a deep breath and spoke more slowly. "Finished? Here, let me take your plate. A few tarts left. Shall

I warm a couple? And what's your preference? Hot coffee or cold milk?"

The next Thursday, while sitting at the bus stop waiting for the twelve-twenty bus that would get her to the university just in time for biology lab, she saw him. Or didn't see him.

Not until he stood directly in front of her.

"Are you buried in that book?"

That voice! Her head jerked up and she saw Brad Vandercamp grinning at her.

"Oh. I...I was reading."

"Obviously." He sat beside her. "You haven't looked up for ten minutes."

"Ten minutes?" she repeated, rather stupidly, wondering what he was doing there.

"Exactly. I've been watching you from across the street."

"You have?" She glanced over to see a silver sports car parked at the curb.

"I almost missed you. You're out of uniform." He scrutinized her jeans and pullover. "I rather like that casual look."

"It's comfortable," she said.

"Well, it quite threw me off. No starched apron, lace cap. If you hadn't had your head bent... Do you know I've never seen a haircut quite like yours?"

Not surprising, since she chopped it off herself.

"There's a certain way your curls fall when your

head is bent. I had passed, but backed up to take a better look.''

''Oh. You were driving?'' On his way to see Whitney, she thought. ''In this area,'' she said.

He nodded. ''You could say that. As a matter of fact, I've been haunting this area for the past week.''

''Oh?'' she asked, puzzled. She knew he hadn't been back to the house. Whitney'd been waiting on pins and needles, and in a foul mood because he didn't show.

''Yes.'' He leaned back and stretched out his legs. ''Decided...or, rather, was forced to take my friend Carl's suggestion, even though I dislike playing stage-door johnny.''

''Pardon?'' What was he talking about?

''Never mind. Tell me, what are you doing so far from where you work? Or don't you live there?''

''I do live there. I'm several blocks away because city transit wouldn't dare traverse the posh lanes of Turtle Cove. I was waiting... Oh, good heavens, I've missed it!'' she cried as she stood too late, and the city bus rolled by.

''Missed what?''

''That bus! You didn't think I was sitting here for my health, did you?'' It was almost out of sight, and there was a whole hour before the next one. ''Darn! I was so busy talking,'' she said, suddenly extremely irritated. Seemed every time she was with this man she lost track of whatever else was going on! ''If you hadn't come along...''

"Don't blame me. You'd probably have missed it anyway." He gestured toward her book. "Must be fascinating."

"It's not fascinating." She didn't like cutting into animals, but if she meant to be a vet—

"So why were you so absorbed?"

"What?"

"If you didn't find it fascinating, why were you glued to each page?"

"One page!" she said, reminded of what was important in her life. "The diagram of a porcine's anatomy."

"A porci...what?"

She grinned at him. "Pig, to you."

"That's what held your interest?"

"We're dissecting pigs today. And now I'm going to miss it. I had it all in my mind, and I'm not even going to be there." She kicked at the curb, furious at him. At herself. Standing like a bedazzled idiot, gabbing with this—this... Playboy was what Lew called him, and he was probably right. *Probably flashes that stupid grin at every stupid woman who*—

"Where to, my lady?"

"What?"

"Wherever you're dissecting this pig, I'll wager I can get you there before the bus would."

"This is nice of you," she said three minutes later as the sleek sports car sped past the bus she had missed. "I'll have time to get set up."

"To cut up a pig," he said, wincing and looking quite puzzled. He glanced at her. "Stargazing, waitressing. Not to mention pigs! Rather diversified interests."

She dimpled. "All connected."

"Oh?"

"Sure. You dream, wish on a star. Then you set out to make that dream come true."

"*That* dream? You made just one wish on all those first stars?"

"Just one. I just wanted...want to be a veterinarian."

"Really? You are a puzzle. The world has gone berserk! There was a time when young women had more...well, romantic dreams, especially if they wished on a star."

"I suppose," she said, surprised herself, now that she thought about it. Maybe because the romantic stuff—Toby, marriage, the ranch—had been pretty well settled. "I guess I thought I had everything else I wanted," she said.

"And now?"

"Now?"

"Do you still have everything you want?"

"Oh." How could one dance, one kiss on a starlit night instill such longings, such disturbing dreams into a life that had been so complacent? Even now, just sitting beside him...

"You haven't answered."

"I'm thinking!" she said, laughing as she tried to

brush away silly romantic notions. "Now... Well, I don't have everything I want, and I've found that wishing won't make it so. That's why I appreciate this ride. I can't miss any of the science classes."

"Especially when you're to cut into a hog."

"Right. From hogs to horses."

"Horses!" He was trying to see her in the role of a vet dealing with small animals. "But... Surely not horses," he said, gripped by a fierce protective instinct. One swift kick of a stallion's hoof could send her small body to kingdom come.

"But I love horses, and I'm very good at dealing with them," she said with a confident smile. "Anyway, that's a long way off. All I have to deal with today is a dead pig."

"And getting back and forth on a bus, working at the Ashfords and with that catering fellow. Does it take two jobs?" he demanded, feeling curiously disturbed as he remembered. *Some of us have to earn our way.*

"Every little bit helps," she said, her smile as complacent as it was bright. "You have to pay for what you want."

Brad, who'd never had to work to pay for anything he wanted, turned this concept over in his mind. The woman beside him seemed to take a certain delight in...well, doing it all for herself.

"Oh, this is great," she said, as he turned onto the campus. "I usually have to run all the way from the bus top to make class on time. Straight down this way and turn left at the next corner. The science building is at the end of that block." When he stopped in front of the building, she was gathering her books. "This was a lifesaver. Thank you."

"How long is this class?" he asked, as she started to get out. "I'll wait for you and—"

"No, don't. It's two hours, and I have another class afterward. I'll take the bus home. You've done your good turn for the day. Thank you and goodbye."

He did not say goodbye. He watched her join the hurrying students and disappear into the building. He wondered where he should park. He wouldn't let her get away this time until he had the answer to a few questions. When and where could he see her again? How could he contact her by phone? Who was that obnoxious gardener who seemed determined that he not see her?

He didn't recall ever having worked so hard for a simple date in his life. Usually a phone call, at the most a dozen roses would suffice. Or not that much, he thought with a chuckle. The difficulty was usually in avoiding a particularly aggressive female or a calculating parent anxious to make a splendid match for a daughter. He had never thought much about it before, but he did know he was considered quite a catch, which brought to mind another puzzling question. Why was he so unsuitable in the eyes of that impertinent gardener? Had the man actually said, "Not about to let her get mixed up with the likes of you"?

And why was it his bloody business, anyway? Brad wondered, as he stopped a jogging student to ask directions to the parking lot. He parked and walked across the campus, barely noticing the slight drizzle that had begun. He was preoccupied with another puzzling question. Why was it so important to see more of this particular woman?

She couldn't believe he was still there. Couldn't suppress the thrill of pleasure that rippled through her to see his eyes eagerly searching, relaxing when he saw her. The collar of his jacket was turned up, and the burnished copper hair was damp from the rain.

"Why didn't you come inside?" she asked.

"Oh, I did. I wandered around and took a good look at the whole place. Even peeped into your lab with all those stinking pigs," he added, wrinkling his nose. "Don't see how you stand it."

"Oh, you get used to it," she said, laughing.

"Well, I prefer the rain. Anyway, I didn't want to miss you in a crowded hall. Thought I'd better come outside and watch the door," he said, shifting her bag from her shoulder to his and taking her hand.

"But it's been over three hours," she said, liking the feel of his hand clasping hers. "I told you not to wait."

"I know. But I'm not about to lose you again."

"Lose me?"

"Right. I thought, once I learned where you lived, finding you would be a simple matter. But when I called at the Ashford residence and asked to see you it proved to be an insurmountable undertaking."

"You— When?"

"Pardon?"

"When did you come and ask for me?"

"At least a week ago. Yes, one week exactly. You were probably, as now, here at school."

"But I thought you came to see Whitney." Whitney had said so herself, as had her mother and Lew.

"I was ushered in to Miss Ashford by mistake."

"Oh." Of course they would take for granted that he had come to see Whitney.

"I didn't correct that mistake because, er..." He hesitated. "Somehow I got the impression that to do so might jeopardize your position."

Indeed it would have, Paula thought, horrified. *If he had asked for me...*

"It should have occurred to me that your employer might object to your receiving callers. Sorry."

Paula had stopped listening. He had come to see her. She took quick steps, trying to match her pace with his. Never had the cool, damp air seemed so refreshing, the leaf-littered campus so beautiful. He hadn't come to see Whitney. He had come to see her! She breathed in the wonder, felt the pang of jealousy that had nagged at her all week fade in its glow.

"You do have time, don't you?"

"Time?" She was in the car, and they were driving out of the parking lot, and she hadn't heard a word he said.

"To have dinner. You don't have to get back right away, do you?"

"No." Thursday evening was clear unless the Ashfords were doing something special or Harry needed her.

"Good. So... You know this town better than I. Where's the best place?"

"Let me think." Her mind reeled with delight that their time together was not yet over. She puzzled over where. Someplace where no one of the Ashfords' ilk would frequent, and far from the campus and intrusion of noisy students.

She settled on the Spaghetti Factory. Perfect. She wasn't out of place in her jeans, and it was almost devoid of customers this early in the evening. As soon as they were seated, they settled into the easy camaraderie they had enjoyed on the deck of his ship. The wine and delicious spaghetti were almost neglected as they skipped from one subject to another, totally absorbed in each other. She told him about her classes and more of her life on the ranch. He talked of England, polo and, yes, he had really bought a ranch. Would she like to see it? When?

She hesitated. She was eager to see it, but between school and work, the problem was when. "I'm not sure when I would have the time. Sunday's supposed to be my day off, but if the Ashfords plan—"

"Sunday it is then! Your day off is yours. The Ashfords don't own you."

"No, but they have been very understanding about my classes. I try to accommodate them, as well." She looked at him, willing him to understand.

His mind seemed to be on something else. "Neither, for that matter, does that damn gardener!"

"Gardener?"

"The Ashfords' gardener. He—" He turned to her as if struck by an idea. "Look, Paula, has that old guy made a pass at you or—"

"Lew!" She couldn't help the gurgle of laughter. "Of course not. He—"

"Well, he's mighty damn possessive. He fired up at me the minute I asked for you and made no bones about warning me to stay clear of you. I thought—"

"Just a minute." She set down her wineglass and gave him a keen look. "Tell me this again. Lew knew that you... You told him that you wanted to see me?"

"I sure did. I did have the good sense to go to the back entrance, and this man was working in the yard. He became quite belligerent when I asked for you. We were having quite a set-to when Mrs.

Ashford appeared, and the chap had the cheek to tell her I had asked for Miss Whitney. I—''

Paula looked through him. Her mind was in the kitchen with Lew, and she was furious! No wonder he had looked so sheepish. Been so awkward. She could wring his neck! He had lied to her. Well, let her think that Brad had come seeking Whitney, and it had made her so miserable she wanted to die. *Just you wait, Lew! Wait till I get hold of you!*

"His attitude to me, a stranger, was incomprehensible. If he has no interest in you himself, then why—"

"He does have an interest in me," she said, her anger gone as suddenly as it had come. Time for truth. *So miserable you wanted to die. Just because a man you had seen only twice in your life visited another woman. Butterflies in your stomach right now just because he's sitting across from you.*

"An interest?" Brad asked, looking anxious.

"Oh, not in the way you think," she said quickly. "He's my uncle, and my godfather, as well. He's always trying to protect me."

"But...from me?"

"I'm afraid so," she said, smiling as she remembered Lew's warnings about rich playboys, and his words, "I don't want to see you hurt, Paula."

"Why?" Brad asked. "Doesn't he want you to have any fun? And what harm is...is this?" he asked, his gesture taking in the wine, spaghetti, the tête-à-tête. "What harm in visiting my ranch? I've bought some riding horses, too. There's a little mare just right for you."

What harm, indeed, she thought, staring at him. She was taking the whole thing too seriously. Like she was in love or something stupid like that. Butterflies? A symptom of the fun she had been missing, buried, as she had been in the past two years, in school and work.

"Wouldn't you like to come out to the ranch? Take a ride on the mare?"

She would! She hadn't been on a horse since she left home. "I'd love to."

"All right. Sunday. Shall I pick you up, or..." He hesitated. "Perhaps you'd prefer to meet me someplace?"

"Yes. That would be best," she said. "Only... I would like you to talk to Lew first."

"Oh? You need his permission?"

"I suppose not. But...well, I'd not like the Ashfords to know that I'm meeting you, but I don't want to deceive Lew. I'd like you to talk with him first."

"To get his permission?"

"No. I could do that myself." She'd always been able to twist Lew around her finger. "But I don't want him to be anxious, and he would be." *Unless he sees for himself that you don't fit his rich playboy image,* she thought. "Unless he gets to know you himself," she said.

"You are a most unusual woman, Paula Grant,"

he said, and his smile was as amused as it was troubled.

"Oh."

"Pretty and provocative. But you do present quite a challenge."

"How is that?"

"Never mind. Where do I beard this lion? In his den or elsewhere?"

CHAPTER SEVEN

"COULDN'T you spare a dollar, buddy?" The man swayed in front of him, reeking of stale whiskey and sweat, murmuring about coffee and a bus ticket.

Brad fished into his pocket, found a twenty and handed it to him. "Get the coffee first," he advised as he moved down a block littered with broken wine bottles and empty beer cans. A man snored peacefully on a nearby bench, and a few loiterers were about, all looking as if they lived where they were.

Brad took a paper from his pocket. Tommy's Tavern, 601 Oceanside. That was where Paula said her uncle was to be found on Friday night, playing a bit of poker with his cronies.

Not as persnickety about his own affairs as he is about his niece, Brad thought, as he threaded his way through the disreputable section searching for the sign.

He found it one block away, across the street, and it was as if he had crossed from a slum into...well, a fairly decent area. Nothing fancy, but more upscale than what he had just walked through. The tavern, a solid three-story building, proved to be a rooming house, eatery and social hall, serving solid working-class citizens, he surmised from the nearby shipping yards. Lew was, as Paula had said he would be, in the card room, a spacious room containing several tables where men and one or two women were gathered, rolling dice, playing cards or just talking and laughing as they sipped their drinks. Just like any other private social club, Brad thought, as he stood in the doorway and listened to the table-to-table quips.

He spotted Lew with six men at a table in a far corner, a stack of poker chips in front of him, seriously studying the cards in his hand. Hesitating to disturb him at this crucial time, Brad went into the adjacent bar and perched on a stool that afforded a clear view of Lew through the open door. He ordered a drink and waited. He had been there for some time, waiting for an opportune moment to approach Grant, when a young man slipped onto a stool beside him. A drifter from across the street, Brad decided, noting the youth's seedy appearance and the way he surreptitiously avoided the eye of the bartender who talked with a customer at the other end of the bar. Brad tried not to notice as the man greedily consumed peanuts and chips from the bowls on the counter. He was about to tactfully offer to buy him a hamburger when a shout startled both of them.

"Get your dirty paws off! This is for customers only!" The bartender removed the containers and dumped the contents. "And you better get the hell outa here 'fore I call the law."

The youth started to hastily withdraw, but Brad caught his arm and addressed the bartender in his most commanding voice. "I beg your pardon," he said. "We are customers."

"You trying to tell me this guy is with you?"

"He certainly is." Brad met the bartender's challenging gaze with one of his own. "I've been waiting for him. We're to, er, discuss a business matter."

The bartender looked doubtful, but Brad was not a Vandercamp for nothing. "I think we'll have a snack while we talk," he said in a tone that demanded instant obedience. "We'll have..." He scanned the menu posted on the wall and ordered the most nourishing selection listed. "Is that all right with you?" he asked the young man.

The man, speechless with surprise, could only nod. But he wasn't too surprised to eat when a steaming plate of chili was set before him.

"Slow down," Brad continued. "You're much too hungry to rush."

"Starving. I don't know who you are, and I know we ain't got no business to talk about, but I sure do wanta thank you. First decent meal I had since—"

"Oh, I don't know that we have no business to discuss. What can you do?" Brad found himself asking. His trainer was setting up a staff at the ranch. There ought to be something this man could do.

Then he saw Grant gathering up his chips. He found the paper in his pocket, scratched out the tavern address and scribbled the phone number at his hotel. "Call me," he said, as he hastily rose and strode into the card room. He waited until Lew had cashed in his chips and was turning from the cashier.

"Mr. Grant, could I have a word with you?"

Lew's astonishment was evident. His gaze swept the room, then focused on Brad. "What are you doing here?"

"Paula said this is where I might find you."

"Well?" The tone and stance were hardly welcoming.

"I'd like a word with you, if I may. A private word," Brad explained, noting that others were giving them a not too complacent surveillance.

Grant also noticed. He shrugged and walked to an empty table in the far corner. "Well?" he repeated, as soon as they were seated.

"Paula suggested this meeting," Brad began.

"Why?"

Brad, awkward in the face of Lew's belligerence, pressed on. "She felt that if you...well, were to know more about me, you might feel more...comfortable about her association with me."

"I know all about you and your kind, and I ain't gonna have you messing with Paula. Got it?"

"Messing with? I resent that term." Brad loosened his collar. Damn it, the man was getting to him! "Nevertheless, isn't that a decision Paula should make? She told me you're her uncle, but she's, what? Twenty-three? Quite capable, I should think, of judging—"

"I don't care if she's a hundred. I been looking out for her since she was a babe and I ain't stopping now. Paula's smart, but not smart enough to know your intentions like I do."

"What do you mean, my intentions! Bloody hell! I like Paula, and she seems to enjoy being with me. All we intend to do is see each other from time to time and—"

"Uh-uh! Now you hear this, young fellow, and you hear it good." Lew pointed a finger to emphasize his point. "I won't have my Paula hanging out with a guy who don't have nothing to do but sit on his money or the backside of a horse just having fun!"

"No!" Brad thrust out his own finger. A chord had been touched. "You hear this! You've made several references to the likes of me, so I must assume you have heard of the Vandercamp money and, more important, Vandercamp Enterprises. If so, you must know that we don't sit on our money. That money is working every day, and so are we!" Brad wasn't sure he had the right to use his father's argument since, unlike his father, he took no part in the business. Never mind. He had caught the attention of the impertinent man across the table. Lew stared at him, and Brad continued. "Do you have any idea of the number of people for which we provide work? Hundreds, thousands, throughout Europe, Africa and other parts of the world, including your own United States. So shut up about me and money." He leaned back, taking a more relaxed position, and nodded at the silent Lew. "Now, let's talk about Paula. You seem to be very fond of her, and rightly so. She is a delightful, sensible, intelligent woman who works very hard. Too hard, as far as I can tell. Why do you object to her having a little fun?"

"I don't." Lew finally found his voice. "What I object to is—"

"Me? Why? I would make sure that she enjoyed herself. She loves horses and says she hasn't been on a horse for some time. I'd like to take her out to see my ranch and ride—"

His discourse was abruptly interrupted by the bartender coming in from the bar, the drifter in hand by the collar, and yelling, "Oh, no, you don't! You're not getting out of here until I get this settled!" He pointed his finger at Brad. "You said this guy was with you, and when I serve you, you walk right out, not so much as a look-see at the bill! You trying to slip out on me?"

"Of course not. I'm right here." Brad stood, reaching into his pocket. "What's the tab?"

"Nine dollars and fifty cents. Including your drink, which you left on the bar." The bartender, still clutching the young man, handed over the bill.

Brad didn't take it. He was digging into his pockets, searching. He stared at what he unearthed—one five-dollar bill and eighty-five cents in change. He thought he had a twenty. He remembered the drunk and cursed under his breath. "Look, let me get a check from my car," he said, trying to remember if there was one. There was usually no need for check or card, the Vandercamp name would suffice. He tried to remember to carry money when he was in the States.

"Uh-uh." The bartender shook his head. "We don't take checks. And you ain't getting outa here, and neither is he. I'm calling the law."

"My dear fellow—"

"Don't dear fellow me! I know a hustler when I see one. I knew you was lying through your teeth when you said he was with you. I ain't gonna let no fancy-dressing, fancy-talking uptowner come in here and con me. Hey, Steve," he called to the interested cashier. "Get on the phone and get—"

"Just a minute." Lew broke in. "I'll take care of this. Give me the bill."

"Oh, Lew." The bartender seemed to notice Lew for the first time. "This guy a friend of yours? Or is he conning you, too?"

Lew's lips twitched. "Wouldn't be the first time," he quipped with a smile, as he took out his wallet and paid the sum with a substantial tip. "We don't want no disturbance in here, do we, Mike?"

"Right." The bartender grunted. "But I hate to see you took in, Lew," he said, releasing the young man and giving Brad a nasty look before going out.

The young man lingered. "Sorry, mister," he said to Brad. "I didn't mean to give you no trouble."

"No problem. Remember. Give me a call."

The man nodded and hurried away.

Lew looked after him, turned to Brad. "Now. You were saying something about your millions?"

"Oh, don't be a smart ass! You'll get yours, and you know it. Thanks," Brad added, feeling sheepish. "I just didn't think—well, I thought I had the money. And, anyway, I'm glad I did it. That guy...nothing but a kid and he was hungry."

"Okay, okay. You owe me twelve bucks. Now, what was that about taking my niece out to your ranch?"

"I thought she might enjoy it."

Lew gave him a keen look. "Paula's mighty special to me."

"I can see that."

"And I'm just a little worried about your intentions. My old man always said the road to hell was paved with good intentions."

"Now listen. I—"

Lew waved his hand. "What's more to the point is Paula's way of throwing her whole heart into everything she does, whole hog or none. I'd hate to have her fall for your act. You know what I mean."

"I know what you mean."

"I don't want her hurt," Lew said. "But yes, she is twenty-three and does know up from down and a charming line when she hears it...I hope." He sighed with resignation but gave Brad a vehement glance. "But...use her, hurt her, and you've had it. Don't forget."

Brad nodded again, knowing that Lew Grant was off his case and knowing what it cost him. "Thank you," he said.

Never in his life had he gone through so much for a simple date. After gaining the uncle's nod, it took another week before Paula could find the time. This was after her one o'clock Monday class, when the Ashfords happened to be dining out. They had come straight to the ranch, but it was already late in the afternoon.

Still, no matter how much trouble or how short the time, it was worth it, Brad thought, as they raced along the bridle path, his stallion keeping pace with Paula's mount. Lew was right about Paula throwing her heart into anything she did. Exhilarating just to watch her. Her face was flushed, her wind-whipped curls dancing, her back as straight as an arrow, and she was laughing, in complete control of the spirited little mare. He had known that just any horse would not do. He had carefully searched until he found Windy. She was a beautiful bay mare, strong, sturdy and as fleet and unpredictable as the wind for which she was named. Paula's kind of horse, he had thought, and he bought her.

A thought struck him. Had he bought the whole damn ranch for Paula?

Surely not. Dan had suggested it. The trainer

thought it a good idea to have a team of ponies stabled in the States, and the southern California area was weather perfect. The ranch was perfect, too. The former riding stable had accommodations for stable hands as well as horses, and plenty of acreage for training corrals. Even a good-size house where Dan had already installed his family.

There was the main house, too, where the former owner had lived. A good size and in good condition. Ready and waiting. He could hire a housekeeper, move in...

Oh? Planning to stick around?

Why the hell not! He hated hotels, and there was no other place he particularly wanted to be.

Since this is where Paula Grant lives?

The thought riveted his attention. He had certainly lingered here. And never had he gone through such paces to secure a simple date. The thought of standing in that tavern, fumbling in his pockets and facing a belligerent Lew was as laughable as it was ludicrous, and—

"Okay, slowpoke. What's so funny?" Paula asked. He realized he had been so lost in thought, he had slowed his pace, and she had dropped back to join him. "Tell me. What's the joke?"

"You."

"Me? You're laughing at me!" she said with mock indignation.

"Not you, precisely. Rather the circumstances surrounding you."

"My circumstances? I assure you, sir, I lead a very circumspect life."

"You're bloody right about that. Shall we take a breather and discuss it?"

"Oh, yes, let's stop here," she said, and immediately turned from the path. "It's lovely here," she said as she slid from her horse. "I didn't know you had a brook."

"One of the things that attracted me," he said, watching the two horses drink greedily from the fresh spring water.

"You were thirsty, weren't you?" Paula said when the mare had drunk her fill.

Brad tethered his stallion but watched Paula. Her face was a rosy glow against the crisp plaid shirt, her figure slender as a reed and enticingly sensuous in those worn, close-fitting riding britches! *Down, boy,* he warned himself, and tried to keep his voice steady. "You look like a real cowgirl in those togs," he said.

"Replicas from the ranch," she said, smiling. "First time I've had them on since I left." She led the mare to a nearby tree. "Thank you, Windy. I loved that ride, and I love you," she said, laying her head against the mare's flank and nuzzling her.

Brad found himself envying the mare.

"And I like your ranch, Mr. Vandercamp," Paula said. She walked to the creek and knelt to dip her hands in the cool water.

"I like you, Miss Grant," he said, sitting beside her, wanting to pull her against him, touch her, kiss her.

"Oh? But you find my circumstances funny, do

you?" She turned a saucy face to him and flipped a bit of water at him.

"Cut it out!" He threw up his hands, laughing. "The joke is on me."

"Oh?" She sat back, hugging her knees, looking even more enticing.

"I'm like Muhammad, trying to make it to the mountain."

"Oh, you! Stop talking in circles. What are you saying?"

"I'm saying that you are the most protected, hard to get to woman I have ever encountered."

"Nonsense."

"You might call it nonsense. But it was by mere chance that I found you when I stumbled into the wrong room that first night. Then I had to wrestle with two formidable employers to find you again, which would have done me no good had you not missed that bus. When I think I've finally made it, you tell me I've got to deal with your bullying uncle."

"Lew's no bully. He's a pushover."

"You think so? Let me tell you about my encounter with him at the little tavern to which you directed me."

"Oh, dear. Was he rough on you?"

"You could say that. He made it quite clear that no one was good enough for you, especially me, scion of that scuttlebutt class, the idle, untrustworthy rich. It was with dire threats should I make an unseemly move that he gave his reluctant acquiescence to our...well, perfectly harmless friendship." By the time he finished, she was lying on the grass, rolling back and forth, laughing her head off. And looking so utterly desirable that he could restrain himself no longer.

"God, you're beautiful," he said, stretching beside her and pulling her close. At last. He touched her. Touched the little tendril of hair that blew against her temple. Kissed her there. Traced light kisses along her cheek, nibbled at her ear. Felt his pulses quicken as she gasped and clung to him. He touched his mouth to the soft curve of her lips, lingering, exploring, tasting the sweetness.

Her fingers dug into his hair, and she gave a little moan. He bent his head to taste the pulse that throbbed at her throat, slipped his hand beneath her shirt, the only barrier to the smooth softness of her bare skin. He cradled the mound of her breast and teased the nipple with his thumb.

"Brad. Oh, Brad," she murmured. He felt her body press against him, yielding, wanting, and knew her surge of desire was as great as his own.

"I know," he answered, feeling an overwhelming need to possess, to be possessed by this woman whose every gesture signaled a willingness to give with all her heart and soul. *Who throws her heart into whatever she does.*

The thought penetrated his brain, but his body burned with desire. She wanted what he wanted. He wouldn't, couldn't let go.

Other words hit him like a dash of cold water. *Use her, hurt her....*

On their heels came a wave of feeling as fierce as it was gentle.

Hurt her? Never!

His arm cradled her in a protective gesture. He kissed her on the nose and buttoned her blouse. "I was about to get carried away, my love. You shouldn't be such a temptress."

She smiled, but he could tell she was puzzled and feeling as awkward as he. As if to cover the awkwardness, she looked away from him to the slowly darkening sky. And quickly sat up. "Look!" she cried. "Quick."

"What?" he asked, trying to follow her gaze.

"That star. It's the first one. You said you'd never wished on one. Now's your chance."

He looked at the pale star, just appearing on the horizon. "Well, now, let's see. I wish—"

She put a finger to his lips. "Don't tell. The wish won't come true. Just repeat after me," she said, dimpling at him. "Starlight, star bright, first star I see tonight. I wish I may, I wish I might, have the wish I wish tonight."

Brad repeated the words, feeling restless and frustrated. Silly game.

What the hell did he wish, anyway?

CHAPTER EIGHT

MRS. Ashford sat at her desk in the upstairs sitting room and peered at Paula. "And yams, I think, just like you did them last year, so light and fluffy they melted in your mouth. Now, let's see. You've ordered the turkey." She tapped a pencil to her list. Mrs. Ashford loved to make lists.

Unnecessary lists, Paula thought. *I know exactly what to get for Thanksgiving dinner, if she'd just tell me how many. I wish she'd get on with it so I can do the shopping.*

They were interrupted by Whitney, who stalked into the room. "He's the rudest man imaginable!" she snapped. "He's not returned even one of my phone calls. I know he got this message because—"

"Maybe *you* don't get the message," Rae crooned, coming in behind her. "Like maybe he doesn't want to talk to you."

Whitney was too immersed in her reflections to get the dig. "He could at least respond. You'd think he'd be glad to come to a home away from home for Thanksgiving dinner."

"He's English," Rae said. "What would he know about Thanksgiving?"

"Oh, everybody knows about that. Anyway, it's

a holiday, and nobody likes to celebrate a holiday alone in a hotel."

Paula's heart gave a lurch. Brad's exact words! They'd had quite an altercation. "No school! Why can't you spend the holiday with me?" She had tried to explain. The Ashfords always entertained during holidays. How understanding they were about her classes. How much she owed, but—

"This is Tuesday, dear," Mrs. Ashford said. "He may have accepted another invitation by now."

"From whom?" Whitney asked. "Except that one time when he was playing golf at the country club, nobody has even seen him."

Because he avoids places that I dare not frequent, Paula thought. *But when I'm not with him, he could go wherever he pleases. And does...I suppose.*

"He's still registered at the hotel, but where he spends his time, nobody seems to know."

I know, Paula thought, feeling a warm flush of joy strain her cheeks. Those moments spent with him were very precious to her. The bus stop had become their meeting place. He drove her to school, waited for her classes to be over and drove her back. All her spare time was spent with him, often at the ranch, walking, riding, inspecting the training corrals, looking over the ponies he had bought. She had never known such pleasure.

As Whitney talked, Paula felt a little guilty. It was not in her nature to be surreptitious about anything. Maybe she was being unfair. But Lew had warned her "The old lady don't like nobody outdoing her girls."

"He was so charming that day he came by. I thought he liked me. I certainly like him," Whitney said, and there was such a look of longing in her face. Paula was surprised by a rush of pity. She felt sorry for any woman who could not share what she shared with Brad. Sit beside him on a corral fence, sharing his pleasure as they watched the trainer putting a new horse through the paces. Walk with him, talk with him, feel his lips upon hers...

Rae's voice broke into Paula's reverie. "What about this skirt, Mother, with this blouse?" She twirled for her Mother's inspection.

"Oh, yes! That's lovely, dear. And with those emerald earrings..."

"I think I'll give him another call. After all, I'm the only woman he has visited since he remained here," Whitney said, with a touch of pride.

"Mighty short visit. And that was three weeks ago." Rae giggled. "Probably got a good look at your sensitive eyes and cut out!"

"That's more than you got from your precious lord! And that skirt's too tight for you. You're getting fat."

"I am not! Mother, do you think—"

"Of course not, dear. You look fine. And never mind about that prince fellow, Whitney," the ever practical Mrs. Ashford said. "I've invited the Alstons and that handsome nephew of theirs. And that Mr. Simmons who was so taken with you at the Atkinses the other night. He's with a very prestigious lawn firm, you know, and they say he's making quite a mark for himself."

Whitney sniffed. "His mark doesn't come anywhere near the Vandercamp millions!"

Paula's pity faded as Whitney stalked from the room. She had a strange urge to put her arms around Brad and hold him. Safe from any woman who couldn't see beyond his wealth.

Paula guided the pickup toward the grocery store, deep in plans. She would do the potatoes today and stow them in the fridge, all ready to pop into the oven on Thursday. She would make the pumpkin pies tonight and the angel food cake tomorrow. If she—

A horn sounded behind her, and she glanced into the rearview mirror. She smiled as she spotted Brad in his sleek sports car. He trailed her into the grocery parking lot and pulled into a slot beside the pickup.

She climbed out of the truck, glowing in the pleasure she always felt at the sight of him. "Hello."

"Hello, yourself," he said as he bent and kissed her full on the lips.

"Oh, don't!" She jerked in alarm. "Someone might see you."

"Let them. I'm tired of this hide-and-seek business." He started to kiss her again, but she darted past him.

"Cut it out, Brad. You're going to get me in trouble. What are you doing here, anyway?"

"Actually I was on my way to see you."

"You were coming to the Ashfords' and... Don't you dare! I told you—"

"I know what you told me. But it's not really pertinent."

"Not pertinent? What are you talking about?"

"I'm talking about an idea I want to discuss with you."

"Well, you picked a heck of a time to discuss it. I've got a billion things to do." She glanced at her watch. "Starting now. I have to pick up these groceries so I can get back in time to—"

"You have to fetch and carry as well as cook?"

"I do if I want the freshest vegetables and potatoes with no bad spots," she said, laughing. "Lew is not too picky."

"Well, you do too damn much. That's what I want to talk to you about."

"Brad, can't it wait? I really don't have time to—"

"No, it can't. We need to thrash this out. I'm pretty fed up with this game we're playing. Now I see you, now I can't."

"Look, if you want to talk, you'll have to trail along. I can't stop." *Not that talking is going to do any good,* she thought as she hurried into the grocery store. She grabbed a shopping cart, took out her list and headed toward the fresh fruits. She wanted to get some oranges and pineapple for the ambrosia. She thought Brad had followed her, but he was so silent. She turned to see him staring like a zombie, eyes agape.

"Brad?" Was something wrong?

He grinned at her "Hey, this is something else, isn't it?"

She looked around. Nothing special. Just the usual crowd of shoppers. The piles of neatly arranged fruit. Shiny apples, carefully sorted—red Delicious, yellow Delicious, fudge, and the little green ones she liked for her pies. The golden, green-tasseled pineapples, the bunches of bananas, purple grapes, the green seedless—

"You just pick out what you want, huh?" Brad made a gesture of pleasure touched with wonder.

"Brad, you act like you've never been in a grocery store before."

"I haven't." He shrugged. "Guess there was no need."

Guess not, she thought. There was always someone else to do it for him.

"Hey, these look good." He picked up a red Delicious. "You want some of these?" Whatever he wanted to talk about seemed to have faded from his mind, and he followed her, taking an enthusiastic delight in helping her.

She smiled. Hadn't she been thinking, just a few minutes before, how simple things gave her a special pleasure when shared with him? But for him, this wasn't just being with her, it was a completely new experience...shopping in a grocery store! Imagine.

"Think you have enough?" he teased, as they went out with two loaded carts.

"Maybe," she said. "I'm preparing for a dozen people."

"Well, this will be the last time," he said.

"What?"

"I've been looking at condos," he said. "There's a really nice one for sale near the university. Perfect for you," he said, as he moved to help the boy put her packages in the truck.

She could hardly wait for the boy to leave them alone. She looked at him. "What is this about a condo?"

"I've found a perfect one for you. When can you see it? I've already talked to the agent, and if you like it—"

"Just a minute! I'm not in the market for a condo. I can't afford it."

"It's not for you to buy. It's for you to live in."

"I have a place to live."

"Yeah, the Ashfords'. Where you work. You don't need to work."

"Oh?"

"Look, this is my idea. I'll buy the flat. You can move in and—"

"And you will provide me with all the little necessities I need like food and bus fare? Maybe this deal includes a shiny new car, too?" She glared at him, her blood running cold. Or maybe it was hot. She was certainly steaming mad!

"Oh, for gosh sake, don't get so hyped up. All I'm trying to do is fix it so you'll have more time—"

"Available for you, huh?"

"More time to study and not have to work so hard. And okay...so we'll have more time together. Now don't look like that! I'm not meaning to move in with you or anything like that. Your uncle could live with you, see? Everything on the up-and-up!"

"Ha! I'd like to see you approach Lew with a proposition like that. He's never accepted a handout from anyone in his life. And neither have I! So you can just take your little flat and stuff it!"

"Paula, you're taking this all wrong. Look, consider it a loan. Just till you get out of school. You can pay me back whenever—"

"I don't owe you anything now and I never will. I've always taken pretty good care of myself, and I'm not about to become a...a paramour, now or ever!"

"Come on! I'm not trying to turn you into anything. I'm just trying to give you a little space. All you do is study and work. No time for fun, much less a little time for me."

"I think I manage my time very well, thank you."

"Well, look at it from my side. I am willing and able to help you through this wicket to become a veterinarian or whatever. With absolutely no strings attached. Remember...no strings attached. None! What's wrong with that?"

She gave a little shrug. "That's life. As Lew puts it, you play with the cards you're dealt. I'm not complaining."

"Well, I am. I'm able, I like you, and I want to help. Don't you see?" he asked, with vehemence.

"Well, maybe I do," she reflected as her anger subsided. "But you don't understand." He really didn't, she thought. A person who'd never shopped in a grocery store... She touched his arm. "Thank you, Brad. That was a generous offer, and I did take it the wrong way. I'm sorry. But I can't accept."

"Why can't you?"

She sighed. "It's hard to explain, but...there are some things money can't buy." *And some things you don't want to sell. Like independence,* she thought.

"That's no answer."

"Yes, it is. You see, when you've worked as hard as I have for something, all of it, even the struggle, becomes a part of you. If I let you take over now, it would be like...well, like selling myself. I'm not for sale, Brad." Impulsively, she stood on tiptoe and kissed his cheek. Then she climbed into the pickup and shut the door.

He watched her drive out of the parking lot, wanting to run after her. He wanted to get in his car and follow her, storm into the Ashford house, shake her until he made her understand.

He took a deep breath, mad at himself. He had handled it all wrong. He had always thought of himself as diplomatic, self-possessed, assured. Smooth, one of his American friends had put it.

So how did you muff this one, buddy?

Not I! She! She's got this bug about doing it all for herself.

Which leaves very little time for you, huh?

Right, he thought, as he got into his car. He was being more selfish than altruistic. How had it happened? He had been attracted to other women, and yes, once or twice quite taken by a particular one. Like...what was her name? Joanne, that time in France. And, skiing in Switzerland, he had been entranced with beautiful blond Zoey...for one whole month. But, to tell the truth, it had always been easy come, easy go.

Never like this, he thought. Just being with her gave him such a lift. Excited, in a way, but also at peace, like he was where he ought to be.

Lonely and bereft when she wasn't with him.

That didn't make sense. He had always been able to lose himself in polo or working with his ponies. Even tennis and golf. But now...well, it was like her absence left a gap, and nothing was as much fun. He'd find himself wondering where she was, what she was doing and...damn it, when the hell would he see her again!

He was in his hotel room, standing at the window, staring at a street filled with cars and busy people who had somewhere to go, something to do, when the phone rang.

He turned quickly. He had asked to have his calls screened, but maybe it was Paula. Or maybe the Ashford woman again. Maybe he should accept her dinner invitation. Paula might be serving and he would get a glimpse—

"Mr. Vandercamp?" It was a man's voice. One he did not recognize.

"Yes. Brad Vandercamp speaking."

"My name is Westley Parker, Mr. Vandercamp. I'm the guy you met...well, you were very kind to at that tavern a few weeks ago. You gave me your card and said I might call you."

"Oh, yes. You're looking for a job."

"No. I have a job, of sorts. Temporary, I hope. But, if I may, I'd like some time with you. There's something I'd like to discuss."

"Oh?" The poor guy probably wanted a handout of some kind. Well, why the hell not? "I'm available. I'm at the Senator. Tonight? We could have dinner here." *The guy is probably hungry, and I've sure got nothing to do.*

"I'm sorry. As I told you, I have this job. My hours are from noon till late. Any time before eleven would be good for me, if you could arrange it."

Brad smiled. What was that line about beggars not being choosers? This beggar was sure choosing his own time. But... "Sure," he said. "Almost any time is okay with me. Breakfast. Eight, eight-thirty in the morning?" The time was settled, and Brad put the phone in its cradle, intrigued in spite of himself. The guy probably had some kind of proposition to put before him. Possibly a con game? But what the hell? He could at least hear him out. He didn't have anything else to do.

CHAPTER NINE

WHEN Brad went down at eight the next morning, the man was waiting in the coffee shop. He looked different than he had that night. Cleaner. Older. His jeans were new, his short-sleeved white shirt was spotless, and his sandy hair was neatly brushed. But the hair was thin and receding, and Brad could see the tired lines around his eyes. This was no kid. *Maybe I didn't really look at him that night,* Brad thought. *No,* he decided, *it's his frame, short and slight like a kid, and he's got a kid's wide-eyed innocent look.*

"Let's sit over here," he said, nodding toward a table. If he was going to be conned, he didn't need an audience. The man slid from the counter stool and followed him.

"How old are you?" Brad asked when they were seated.

"Thirty-five."

Older than I, Brad thought. "You sure had me fooled. I thought... But, no matter. What's on your mind, Mr—Parker, did you say?"

"Yes. Westley Parker. I've got a bit of a problem. You see—" He broke off when Brad held up a hand as a waiter approached. Brad ordered his usual full breakfast, but Parker only wanted coffee.

"Aren't you hungry?" Brad asked when the waiter withdrew.

Parker smiled. "Not this time. I get fed at my job."

"Which is?"

"Waiter at the Steakhouse. Been there two weeks. Twelve to three for lunch, five to eleven for dinner. That's why I wanted to talk to you this morning."

"I see. You have a job. But you still have a problem."

Parker nodded. "I'm locked out of my house, my shop."

"But..." Parker didn't look homeless.

"Oh, I got a room. But I need to get back in my shop. It's urgent. And when I looked at the card you gave me...well, the name Vandercamp... Wait, let me explain," he said quickly as he took in Brad's expression. "I better begin at the beginning. You see, I'm an electronics engineer."

Brad's brows lifted. Now he knew he was being conned. He waited until their coffee was poured before he signaled the man to continue. "Yes, I think I'd better hear this from the beginning."

"You can check it out, Mr. Vandercamp. Up until a year and a half ago, I was employed at Cal Electronics. They're right here on Bassett Street. They're mainly into computers, and I'm good at circuit boards, programming, that sort of thing."

"Sounds like a pretty substantial situation," Brad said, looking at the appetizing platter of ham, scrambled eggs and hash browns before him. He hadn't realized how hungry he was. Hadn't eaten anything last night. How could he get so upset over one woman! Well, it was good to have something else to think about. "So what happened?"

"I left the company when my father died, leaving me a legacy. Just his insurance and what I got from the sale of his house in L.A. Not much, but I thought it was enough."

Brad cut into the ham. "Enough for what?"

"This idea for a miniature scanner had been bugging me for a long time. Now was my chance. I could set up shop. Buy the tools."

"Wait just a minute. You're telling me you're an inventor?"

"Oh, sure. I've always fiddled around making things. Made a pinball machine when I was about sixteen. Even developed a few things while I was with Cal, mechanical toys, computer games, things like that."

"Interesting."

"Yes. Anyway, I became particularly interested in voice synthesizers, and I'm trying to develop a scanner."

"A what?"

"A scanner. For blind people. There's one that's already been developed. You stick this paper in a machine and a magnetic voice reads the print back to you. Very slow and very awkward. I'm making a small one that—"

"Wait. You say one has already been developed. At Cal?"

"No. Cal's not into scanners. I could have suggested it, but..." He hesitated, giving Brad an intense look. "Haven't you ever wanted to do something on your own? Something that you alone developed, owned, put on the market?"

"Well..." Brad tried to think. Had he ever wanted to make anything?

"I'm calling it the Parker Scanner. For my father. He went blind and had to retire early."

"That must have been rough."

"Oh, they did okay. Mom worked at Penny's, and he had social security. And you know something? He'd been an auto mechanic, and blind as he was, he could build an old car engine from the bottom up. But he always loved to read, and... Oh, he had the talking books. But current material, newspapers and the like weren't always available. And after Mom died and I left home, it was hard. He'd have to get a neighbor to read his mail, even his social security check. No privacy. Pretty tough going."

"I can imagine."

"If he'd had my scanner... Still a few snags, but I've almost got it!" There was that small-boy wonder in Parker's eyes as he began to describe it. "It's small enough to hold in your hand. You just run it across the page at your own pace, and the magnetic voice picks it up, reads it to you. Newsprint, check, love letters, whatever. A whole new private world for people who lose their sight. Can't you see it?''

His enthusiasm was catching. Brad, whose acquaintance with computers, much less voice synthesizers, was pretty scanty, stared at him, fascinated. "You've made a...a thing that'll do that?"

Parker nodded. "Yes. Like I say, a few snags, but they can be ironed out. Only... Well, I'd like to get on with it.'' He looked earnestly at Brad. "That's why I wanted to talk to you. The thing is, I'm locked out of my house."

"Evicted?"

"Yes. When I got this money from Pop, it enabled me to set up shop. But market and production costs were much greater than I had thought. A bank loan has proven almost impossible, since my item has no track record. So bills became delinquent, and finally my rent, and the shop and all have been impounded. I've been evicted. I just got so involved in what I was doing, and to tell the truth, I've never had much business sense. Anyway, I didn't know I had run out of money until my checks started bouncing, and I was evicted."

"I see. So that night at the tavern—"

"I'd been on the street for a week. Well, not exactly on the street. I'd been sleeping in my car, but I was pretty hungry."

"There was no one to whom you could apply? You must have friends."

"Not really. I'm pretty much of a loner. Even so, you don't want to tell anybody that you've been kicked out."

"Well, you've got a job now. But... If you're an electronics engineer, why are you waiting table? Couldn't you go back to Cal?"

"I told you. This pocket scanner is my idea, and I'm pretty close. I don't want to get involved with another company. This scanner is a revolutionary idea, and it's only a starter. I have ideas that I am convinced would support a firm of my own."

"I see."

"I can still do it. Working like I am, I still have my mornings free. The only thing is..."

Here it comes, Brad thought, seeing Parker's hesitation. "You need money."

"Right. I need to get back into my house. My shop, everything is there, and I'm scared to death somebody might fool with it. My landlord says not. He's got padlocks on, and he's being pretty decent. The stuff in there doesn't mean a thing to him, and he's given me a month to pay up. But it's already been three weeks and, well, even with my tips, I'll never make it."

"How much?"

"Five thousand. More, if I'm to keep the place, which I'd like to. I'd have to start all over again...first and last month's rent, and security, plus what I already owe."

"I see...maybe. Let's go see your landlord," he said. "I'd like to take a look at your place."

The landlord was a portly, amiable man who seemed relieved to receive Brad's check.

"I hated to do this to you, Parker," he said. "You've been a good tenant. But I've got the mortgage to pay, and when a guy gets three months behind," he added, looking at Brad, "well, it really puts me in a bind. But all's well that ends well, isn't it?" He looked at Parker. "I did give you time, and like I said, nothing's been touched."

Parker said yes, and he was grateful, but couldn't they get on out to the house? "Mr. Vandercamp's anxious to see the place," he said.

"He's the anxious one," the landlord said to Brad, when Parker rushed ahead of them as soon as the padlock was removed. "Worried about that junk he's got up in the attic. No need. Nobody's been here. He installed burglar alarms himself when he first moved in, and as you see, I had everything locked tight. Everything okay, Parker?" he asked as Parker came down looking flushed.

"Seems so. Thanks," Parker answered. "Come on up and take a look," he said to Brad when the landlord departed.

Brad followed him up. The attic covered the whole area of the rather small nondescript house, and this was where Parker had set up shop. *What's in it is too well organized to be called junk,* Brad thought, as he looked around. Two long tables, on one of which were three computers, one disassembled. Small intricate tools, hanging or neatly arranged on shelves. Trays containing small objects unidentifiable to Brad.

For a while, Parker was too busy inspecting the premises to notice Brad. However, after satisfying himself that all was in order, he opened a small safe that Brad hadn't noticed and took out what looked like a small camera.

"This," he said, "is the Parker Scanner. Watch." He took a folded newspaper, focused the scanner on the print and switched it on. As a tiny beam of light traversed the page, a voice sounded out the printed words. Garbled and a bit indistinct, but yes! It was picking up whatever the beam focused on.

"Amazing," Brad said, hardly able to believe it.

"Yes. Needs a more finely tuned voice disk. But I can work that out. And then..." He looked at Brad. "So. What do you think?"

"Amazing," Brad repeated, too stunned to express what he felt. This little man had actually made a tiny device that could—

"Well, I owe you. What're you asking?"

"Asking?"

"Look, you just planked down five thousand dollars."

"Oh, that. Well, you can pay it back whenever. I hadn't thought—"

Parker shook his head. "You haven't got much

business sense, either. No promissory note. Nothing."

Brad grinned. "To tell the truth, I'm relieved to find out this isn't a scam. And..." He looked at the man who had spent almost two years constructing the thing. *All I've done is shell out a few thousand, which doesn't mean a thing to me.* "Look, I trust you," he said. "You can pay me back whenever. Glad I could help out. You've got a remarkable device there."

"Damn right, it's remarkable. It's also a moneymaker. And you've just invested five thousand."

"Oh. I see what you mean." Brad wanted to laugh. His father was the investor, not he. Investments, this moneymaker or that, were the only table talk when his father was home. Brad had never been interested. What was the use of making money when he already had more than he could ever spend? What he'd given Parker had been to help out a guy who really needed a boost. He hadn't meant to invest.

"The Angels were going to ask fifty percent."

"Angels?"

"When I found I was running out of money, I tried to find a backer. The banks or the big investors won't even look at you unless you're dealing with a million or more."

Brad nodded. The multimillion-dollar sign had to cap any market or merger for Vandercamp consideration.

"So I tried the Angels. They're a group who have banded together to finance small projects and are supposed to be philanthropists as well as profiteers. That is, if you call fifty percent philanthropic."

"And they weren't interested?"

"There are others working on this same idea, and I guess they thought someone else was closer."

"I see."

"So it looks like you're my angel and I'm ready to sign whatever you think fair. You saved my life. Only let's agree quickly. I've got to get to work."

"Now, just a minute." Brad was a Vandercamp. He might not have been interested in investment talk, but he knew all about it. "If I'm going to invest in a guy, I can't have him wasting his time waiting on tables. The first thing you'd better do is quit that job. And let's talk real business. If we're going to launch this device, much less a whole electronics firm, you're going to work full-time, and you're going to need more than five thousand. And you're going to need help." Parker might be an electronics genius, but he was no businessman.

Brad's mind worked rapidly. He'd talk to the family lawyer, have him recommend a good patent lawyer. Check with a real estate agent to search out a site for a decent plant.

Brad went to work right away. He accompanied Parker on his sessions with the patent lawyer. Inspected the sites the agent recommended. They found an abandoned warehouse near a naval base.

The warehouse would have to be torn down, but the site was perfect. As he negotiated the sale, he suddenly realized he was having fun. The patent lawyer had assured him the scanner was a revolutionary item that would bring in a bundle, and it was not the only item Parker intended to produce and market. Brad found he was as excited as Parker about the forthcoming Parker Electronics.

He also realized he was out of his depth. Necessary production and office space must be assessed before any building plans could be made. Parker, who was closeted in his attic workshop perfecting his pocket scanner, was no help. Brad decided that, before he did anything else, he'd best hire a company executive. Someone who could consult with Parker and an architect, accept bids and decide on contractors. He'd have to be experienced and capable.

He'd better consult...who else? His father.

Bradley Elmwood Vandercamp, Senior, was thunderstruck. "You're doing what!"

Brad explained, leaving out how he happened to become acquainted with Parker. No, he hadn't touched the trust Grandfather had left him, nor given some bum a blank check. His share in the company? Twenty-five percent. "Seems fair to me," he answered to his father's complaint. "It is Parker's brainchild. Yes, Father. Everything is in order," he said, getting impatient. Did his father take him for a dunce? "I had Diggsby check it out."

The fact that his own lawyer had been consulted and had given his approbation seemed to satisfy the elder man, and he opened up with enthusiasm and more advice than Brad needed.

Brad replaced the receiver, thinking that was probably the longest conversation he had ever had with his father. But he held in his hand a list of three men, any one of whom, he had been assured, had the expertise he needed. He contacted them immediately and arranged for interviews.

It had been two weeks since he'd seen or heard from Paula. But this, he thought, he'd like to share with her, and took a chance that she'd be at the bus stop, as usual. She was! He was bursting with his new venture, and he tried to fill her in as they drove to the university.

"Parker is beside himself," he concluded. "And he has a right to be. He's a genius. Imagine developing such a contraption! It looks like a small camera you could hold in one hand. You just focus it on a page, and this magnetic voice picks up every printed word as you move it along. Amazing."

"And he constructed it all by himself? In this little attic workshop?"

"Yes."

"But he needed someone to finance the project?"

"Right."

"So how did he contact you? Oh, I suppose, the Vandercamp name?"

"Well, yes, in a way. But he had met me. Funny

thing," he said, grinning at her. "You're responsible for the introduction."

"Me?"

"Uh-huh. Remember you sent me to that tavern to, er, confer with Lew?"

She nodded.

"Well, Lew was quite occupied, and I didn't want to break up his game. I was waiting at the bar, and this kid came in. At least, I thought he was a kid. Anyway, he was filching condiments from the bar, which the bartender didn't take too well. Anybody could see the guy was hungry."

"So you staked him to a meal."

"I was going to, but... Actually it was Lew." He glanced at her. "Didn't he tell you?"

She shook her head.

"I thought he would. He got such a kick out of me being out of funds."

"You're kidding!"

"I kid you not," he said, laughing. "But protocol prevailed. We of the British aristocracy may at times be short of cash, but never, and I repeat never, are we without our calling card. I gave the gentleman my card, thinking job."

She laughed with him. "I see. And that's how he found you."

"Yes. So if you hadn't made me go to that tavern... Lucky night for me."

"Sounds like a lucky night for Mr. Parker..."

"Maybe. But he's so grateful. And, truth to tell,

the whole thing gives me a kind of lift. These past two weeks...well, it's like I'm participating in something innovative and quite remarkable. It's a good feeling."

Paula studied him as he maneuvered the car through the crowded university streets. This was the polo prince, acclaimed internationally for his skill at the game, probably more for his wealth and family background. He was featured in the tabloids, the rich, handsome, charming Brad Vandercamp, the most eligible bachelor in the world. Admired. Sought after. He had it all.

And yet... She had never seen him so excited, she thought. About something someone else had done. Discounting himself, even his own considerable contribution to the project.

"I like you," she said when he stopped at the science building. She touched his arm, smiling at his what-brought-that-on expression. "You're a very special person, Brad." She blew him a kiss as she slipped from the car. She hurried into the building, deliriously happy that he would be waiting for her.

CHAPTER TEN

"No, I CAN'T go out to dinner tonight," she said when they got in the car and started back. "Mrs. Ashford is having a dinner."

"You see! That's what I've been talking about." Brad sounded irritated, as she had known he would be. "You rush here. Your class must be pretty grueling. Now you've got to rush right back, fix a dinner for...how many?"

"Only eight. No big deal. I set it up before I left. All I have to do now is—"

"Rush back and knock yourself out like you always do. All set up, huh? Knocked yourself out before you left, didn't you?"

"Brad, listen. I want to tell you—"

"No, you listen. Paula, this doesn't make sense. Your working like this when I could—"

"Brad! We've been through that. Please, don't start again."

He shrugged and concentrated on his driving as he turned onto the freeway.

"Don't you want to hear what I have to tell you?" she asked, trying to coax him into a better mood.

"What?"

"It's a...well, a kind of Christmas present."

"A bit early, aren't you?" He flashed her a smile. "A Christmas present for me?"

"For...for both of us. At least I hope you consider it a present," she said, faltering. Maybe he wouldn't. He might already have plans for Christmas, back in England or anywhere. After all, he was Brad Vandercamp, and—

"Well, come on. What is it?"

"A week. Maybe ten days. The Ashfords are spending the holidays in Connecticut with a cousin, and I thought..." She hesitated, suddenly shy. "I'll have lots of free time, and I thought we could spend it together. Most days, anyway. That is, if you'd like."

"If I'd like!" He turned to her, grinning. "I'd love it! We could—"

"Brad, watch! That truck."

"I'm watching. I'm watching," he said, and she breathed a sigh of relief as he slowed down and allowed the big truck to whiz by. "What do you mean, most days? We'll spend the whole week at... Let's see. Where would you like to go?"

"Nowhere. I can't," she said. *I'm not ready,* she thought. *Not ready to be one of the train of women whom he dated, dined, took on trips. Not ready to be one of the anxious gullible women who yearned to be the one.*

Well, you did yield to the dining and dating, didn't you?

Yes, but... She tried to explain it to herself. It was like he invited her to...well, to flirt and have a little fun. And she was having fun.

She had not really thought of it before, but she had never dated anyone but Toby. She had loved Toby, and his desertion had left her in a fog so dense she had not looked at anyone else. Then she had lost herself in school and work. Until Brad.

"Hey, wake up!" he said. "Didn't you hear me? Good Lord..." He broke off to wrestle with the peak-hour traffic. "Where is everybody going in such a rush?"

She hadn't heard him, so stunned was she by a revelation. She hadn't loved Toby. He had just been a comfortable habit. No wonder she had felt like the ground slipped from under her when he deserted her. A habit. Not love.

A habit that had left her inexperienced and inexplicably vulnerable to someone like Brad. She had never been around anyone quite like Brad. It was...well, like being in some new and exciting foreign territory. Wonderfully exhilarating...and dangerous.

"Why can't you?"

"Oh! Well, I...we have to house-sit." Not exactly a lie. Lew had to house-sit. Ordinarily she would go home, and her parents were wondering why she wasn't coming. But when she found she had the time, all she had thought of was Brad. Time to be with him.

"Can't Lew house-sit?"

"He could. But I don't like to leave him alone. And...well, I really have some studying to catch up on."

"So we really won't have all that time together, after all, will we?" he said as he turned onto the avenue and approached the bus stop, their point of departure.

"I guess not," she said, her spirit sagging. Why would he stick around dull San Diego when there were more glamorous places to be? More glamorous women to be with?

"Even so... We'd have more together time than we have now, wouldn't we?"

She nodded, feeling her pulse quicken.

"Christmas Day?"

"Oh, yes!"

"Promise?"

"Of course. I'll get a tree." She was already decorating Lew's garage apartment. "I'll fix dinner at Lew's."

He pulled to a stop, shaking his head. "No, at my hotel. Or better still, the ranch!"

"Could we? Oh, Brad, that would be perfect." Almost like being at home, she thought. And with Brad. She could hardly contain herself. She wanted to linger with him and plan, but she had a dinner to prepare right now. "We'll talk later," she said, forcing herself to get out of the car.

She danced on light footsteps all the way to the

house while wonderful exhilarating expectations danced in her head. Little signals about dangerous foreign territory faded from her mind as she contemplated the pleasure of his company, free and unhampered for seven heavenly days.

Pure joy.

She didn't see Brad again until the following Saturday, exactly one week before Christmas Day. The Ashfords had departed the evening before, and she felt more free than she had felt in a long time. Wonderful to be at no one's beck and call.

"You're an early bird," she told Brad when he came to take her out to the ranch. He had said in the morning, but she hadn't expected him before nine.

"I don't plan to miss one minute of our vacation. Besides, I have something to show you."

"You've bought another pony."

He smiled. "No. Something quite different. I hope you'll like it."

"I like this," she said, as he helped her into the car. "I feel like a princess, being picked up at the house so openly, in broad daylight."

"That's the way it ought to be. You shouldn't have to sneak. They don't own you."

"I know. Still..." She glanced at the nearest neighbor's house as they passed. "I hope no one sees us," she said with a little chuckle.

"I hope they do," he said. "And I hope they talk. Then maybe this game will end."

"Don't you dare wish such a thing! Not yet. Give me eight more months."

"What happens in eight months?"

"I'm thanking Mrs. Ashford very much and bidding her goodbye."

"Excellent idea! Why wait eight months?"

"Because I need the work," she said. "And the compensation. Free room and board, which is why I took the job in the first place."

He stared at her. "You don't mean that's all you're getting for—"

"Look where you're going, Brad! Of course not. I receive a decent salary, some of which I manage to save. It will come in handy next year when I'm a clinician."

"What's a clinician?"

"Veterinary parlance for what is an intern in the medical field." She turned toward him, glowing at the thought.

"That's what I'm going to become next fall. I'll be in the veterinary hospital, actually working with the animals. On call sometimes at night. That's why I won't have time for any other job next year. And, since my specialty is horses... Oh, Brad, you're going to love this!"

"Oh?" He wouldn't love it, not if it had to do with her doctoring horses. She was an expert horsewoman. But riding them was one thing, doctoring them was another. He just couldn't conceive of her lifting a horse's leg or jabbing a needle into some huge wary stallion or, heaven forbid, cutting into the tough hide of—

"Next quarter, I'm taking equine exercise physiology. I can't wait. I might be helpful to Dan, you know, as he starts to train your new ponies."

"Great," he said, not wanting to dampen her enthusiasm. But Dan was training polo ponies before she was born. Brad doubted he needed her help. Time to change the subject. "I'm making progress on the Parker project."

"Oh? You've hired a real administrator?"

"Not yet. I'm holding off until I talk to the last one. Both the first two were excited about the scanner, but both engaged."

"Unavailable?"

"Oh, either could probably be pried loose, but it might take time and some doing. I like the look of the last one, Ellis Andrews. He's older, retired, but for some reason anxious to get back to work. He's due here Monday."

"Now? In the midst of our—" She broke off and quickly amended, "This is holiday time!"

He grinned. "Now you know how I feel when you get too involved to see me. Don't worry, love, it'll be a very short interview. I'm really getting the hang of this business." He had learned much of what he needed to ask, he thought, during the interviews with the other two men.

When they reached the ranch, Paula was surprised that Brad did not take the route toward Dan's place and the paddocks. He turned instead into the driveway that led up an incline to a spot some distance away where the former owner's house was located. He had pointed it out to her, but she had never been near it. He had not said much about it, and she had been only interested in his horses. And him.

Of course. Where else? He had said the house was empty, but they could bring in a tree, and... She thought of decorating. Lots of holly and mistletoe in the woods, and they could set candles all over the place, put a fire in the fireplace even if it was as warm as all get-out for December. It wouldn't look so empty then. They'd probably have to have a picnic lunch or go back to Lew's for a real Christmas dinner, after all, she was thinking as he led her up the steps, across the old-fashioned porch, through a wide entry hall, into a spacious combination living and dining room. She caught her breath. Empty?

This house was beautifully, lavishly, completely furnished. *At least this room is,* she thought, surveying it.

What gives it that warm inviting lived-in-for-years look? she wondered. *Is it the way the warm, rich colors of autumn have been so subtly blended? This,* she decided, as she sank into the soft comfort of one of the sofas and ran her hand over the smooth cushions. *Or this, the clever arrangement of furniture in cozy conversational settings, the placement of each picture or ornament in just the right place.*

She looked up to see that Brad was regarding her anxiously. "Don't you like it?" he asked.

"Of course I like it! It's just that I'm... awestruck! You said this house was empty."

"It was. A week ago."

"You did all this in just one week!" She thought of a house standing bare and neglected. The relative isolation, at least quite a distance from San Diego and furniture stores.

"Not me. A Ms. Sorenson from Sloane's."

Sloane's, the place for the finest, the most expensive furniture.

"No problem. The house was clean and basically in good condition. Wasn't that fortunate?"

"Very fortunate," she said, looking at the polished hardwood floors dotted with small plush carpets in just the right places.

"I brought her out and told her what I wanted."

And handed her a sizable check, she thought. No problem. Just money.

"And that I wanted it done right away. You didn't think we'd have to camp out, did you?"

"No." But that was exactly what she had thought. A reminder of the distance between herself and Brad Vandercamp.

"Anyway, I had been toying with the idea of

setting up residence here. It's time I had a little place of my own."

A little place of my own. Where he might drop in from time to time, as he dropped in at one family residence or another. The thought seemed to magnify the distance between them.

"You don't like it. I can tell," he said, sitting beside her.

"But I do! I do!" She spoke quickly, not wanting to dampen his enthusiasm. "It's lovely!"

"But something is bothering you," he said. "What would you like to change?"

"Nothing! Not one thing. It's perfect!" How could it be anything but perfect? Just an average, slightly old-fashioned farmhouse. But it now bore the Vandercamp stamp. Like his yacht, she thought, remembering what she had seen of it. The same style, comfort and elegance that only money could buy.

"Then," he said, taking her hand, "what's the matter?"

She didn't know. She couldn't put a finger on a prickling, unsettling sensation that was beginning to surface. "Nothing's the matter. I...I'm just amazed that you could...that so much could be accomplished in so short a time."

"You haven't seen it all," he said, pulling her up. "Come."

She was even more amazed as he led her through the house. No detail had been forgotten. There was china and crystal in the buffet, every utensil and appliance needed in the well-stocked kitchen, guest towels in the small powder room off the entry hall.

And upstairs... Goodness, the former owner must have been no pauper himself, she thought, for each of the four bedrooms had its own private bath. Each bedroom had been beautifully decorated. Towels and linens were in abundant supply, and here, too, no item had been forgotten, from proper bedside lamps to soap dishes in the bathrooms.

"Your Ms. Sorenson must be a miracle worker," she said.

"She is," he replied. "Too bad she couldn't supply a staff. I'm still bunking at the hotel."

Another residence. A staff to cook, clean, fetch and carry. Clearly this was a man not accustomed to roughing it.

"Not to worry," he said. "I'm already interviewing people. By Christmas—"

"No. Don't!" she cried, startling him. "Don't hire anyone. Not till after Christmas."

"But..." He looked puzzled. "I thought you'd like everything in order. Someone to do the dinner, and—"

"I don't want anybody to..." To take away Christmas, she thought. She had always loved Christmas. Loved tramping through the woods to find the right tree, loved gathering the pine cones, holly and mistletoe. Loved the decorating, filling the house with the scent of pine and burning candles. Loved the feel of cookie dough and sugar on her fingers, the smell of things baking in the oven. Nobody could hand her that on a silver platter! "I thought...well, I thought we could be by ourselves," she said.

His eyes softened, understanding. "Yes. Privacy. That's why I wanted everything furnished. Convenient for you to spend a night, or the whole week, if you... Lew too," he added quickly when she pulled away.

"We can't. I told you. We have to house-sit."

"Oh. Anyway, I should have explained. There are quarters for servants behind the house. They won't hover."

He didn't understand. "It's... That's only part of it. It's... Oh, I just like to do things myself." How could she explain that half the pleasure was in the doing? Distance between a woman who had always and a man who had never, well, roughed it, she thought.

"But you're always the doer!" he said. Her look made him relent. "All right. No servants. I'll have a caterer send in Christmas dinner."

"Oh, no! Please. Not just for the three of us." She almost laughed. She could do it with one hand tied behind her back. How many times had she helped Mom do dinner for twenty on Christmas Eve at the big house? And almost that many in their little cottage on Christmas Day. A snap, after weeks of preparation. And all part of the fun, the games, the laughter. Christmas.

"Let's go find a tree," she said. "And I think I saw mistletoe growing on a tree by the lake."

CHAPTER ELEVEN

THE days that followed were strangely different from past holidays. But then, Brad thought, any time spent with Paula was like being in a different world.

Take the matter of the Christmas tree. It certainly wasn't the first time he had walked through his own land to find the perfect tree. As a child, he had often followed Swen and a couple of other gardeners through the Balmour woods to find the right tree. No, trees. A tall one that would tower almost to the twenty-foot ceiling of the front parlor. A not-so-large one for the servants' hall. An even smaller one for his playroom. He would watch the men measure to be sure each tree had the right dimension for the area it would occupy. He might have even lingered to see it cut down and hauled to the house. More often he would desert to chase squirrels or climb trees. Just watching became boring.

He soon grew tired of watching the crew of professional decorators who would come with boxes of lights and ornaments to place the sparkle of Christmas upon the huge manor house. He couldn't remember, but he supposed he must have been excited about the toys Father Christmas placed under the tree to add to his already abundant storehouse.

He knew that, as he grew older, he soon became bored with the festivities, the giving and receiving of gifts, the round of parties where exquisitely clad friends met and mingled, touched champagne glasses and wished each other Merry Christmas.

He had long ago deserted Christmas at home for skiing in Switzerland, polo in Argentina or cruising in the Mediterranean. Different places, different people, somehow all the same, who met and mingled for a not-so-merry Christmas. Boring!

He was never bored when he was with Paula. He didn't understand it. Playing a hard game of polo or gliding down a Swiss mountain on skis and enjoying a hot toddy afterward in company with an alluring partner should be more exciting than chopping down a tree. Certainly easier, he thought, as he struggled with the one she gloated over.

"Yes! This one! See how the branches spread, and we'll put the star right there."

The thing was, he had never before cut down a tree. But it was a small one, and he managed to fell it and bring it to the house with only a little help from Dan. He and Paula had fit it into the stand in which she poured sugar and water, "To keep it fresh and smelling all piney." They had rearranged the furniture to put it in just the right spot. They had gathered Christmas greenery, arranged, tacked and hung it all over the place. Together they had scoured the discount houses for lights, ornaments and candles, which together they placed in just the right spots.

There were short pauses for a picnic lunch in the kitchen or hamburgers from a stand they happened to pass. Lots of laughter. Quick hugs of delight at some minor accomplishment. Kisses...a light peck on the cheek or enticingly full on his lips, hurried but promising. Driving him wild with longing.

"Almost like Christmas at home," she said the evening they finally finished decorating.

"All that's missing is the snow outside and a roaring fire inside."

"Nothing is missing when we're together," he said.

This brought a smile to her lips. "You're right. And I couldn't expect snow and roaring fires in southern California, even in December."

"We aim to please," he said, and promptly struck a match to the gas logs in the fireplace. They gave off little heat but did enhance the setting.

"Good," she said, joining the game. "We'll pretend it's snowing outside. Now...off with the house lights and on with Christmas!

"I like it," she said, when this was done and they sat on the floor before the fire to survey their handiwork. "But then, I always liked it." She gave a little gurgle of laughter. "As soon as the tree was up, the lights turned on and the candles lit, it was like a signal that Christmas was beginning. I'd get this special feeling."

"What kind of feeling?"

"Just a happy, expectant, all is right in my world feeling," she said, smiling. "I'd get all warm and mellow inside, knowing that something wonderful was going to happen. Did you ever feel like that?"

"I do now," he said, transfixed by the glow in her eyes, the flush that stained her cheeks, the tantalizing, inviting curve of her lovely lips. Just looking at her made him feel all warm and mellow inside. He took her into his arms with a sure knowing that something wonderful was about to happen.

The instant and eager rapture of her response signaled that he was not to be disappointed. She was as stirred as he. She wanted what he wanted. He knew it by the way she pressed closer to him, the way her fingers tore at his hair as he deepened the kiss. When his lips traveled down to taste the soft skin in the hollow of her throat, he felt the painful throbbing of her pulse, heard the sensuous gurgle of her pleasure. When his hand slipped under her shirt to caress the small mound of her breast, she did not resist. As his thumb teased the nipple, she clung to him in unmistakable welcome. Her irrepressible erotic gasps of delight ignited the fire of passion smoldering within him. A burning, tantalizing fever of desire possessed him, and—

He almost lost his balance when she abruptly pulled away and stood up.

He looked at her, his breath coming in short, hard

gasps as he tried to gain control of himself, tried to still the urgent throbbing in his groin.

"I...I'd better go," she said. "It's getting late."

As if she hadn't slapped his face. No—worse!

He tried not to look foolish as he finally managed to stand. "Did I get my signals crossed?" he asked, glaring at her.

"Not you. Me. I'm sorry. I didn't mean to... to—" She bit her lip.

"To give out the wrong signal?" he prompted.

"I didn't mean to," she repeated.

"Well, you could have fooled me," he said, ready to lash out at her. To tell her what he thought of that kind of come-on when she did not intend to go the route. "I had thought you too honest to..." He stopped, noticing the awkward fumbling of her fingers as she tired to adjust her blouse. His mood softened. Perhaps he had been too hasty. He had no right to rush her. If she wasn't ready, she wasn't ready. He'd have to respect that. Accept it, even if it was driving him crazy. "Come," he said. "I'll take you home."

Without another word, he walked her to the car, helped her in and drove away from the ranch. Paula glanced at him out of the corner of her eye as he pulled onto the freeway. He didn't look angry. Just passive, unsmiling and silent, seemingly completely absorbed in driving.

She wanted to break the silence, but for the life of her she couldn't think what to say. She had said she was sorry. She had said she didn't mean to lead him on.

Lead him on, for Pete's sake! It was she who was being led...by her body. Her nerves had tingled with eager expectancy, her pulse pounded, and the wild, tumultuous yearning swirling through her had been so intense that she was more than ready to yield to the promise. To fully savor the new and most exciting, exhilarating, powerfully erotic sensations she had ever experienced.

Foreign territory.

Stupid thinking. There was nothing foreign about a man, a woman and sex. Because that's what it was. Sex.

Only... Had she ever felt that way with Toby?

She thought about it. Toby, a childhood habit. Racing on horseback, sailing on a raft, a few kisses. A little petting, but not much. On the ranch there had always been strict parental supervision. By the time they were in college and ready for more heavy petting, they had begun to drift apart. After their separation, for her there was a brief session of what she had thought was heartbreak before she buried herself in school and work.

Good Lord, was she twenty-three years old and so inexperienced that a deeply passionate kiss by any man could...

No. Not any man. Brad.

She stole another glance at him. He was still unsmiling and silent. She couldn't bear to think what he was thinking. That she was an unsophisticated little snot who put too much emphasis on a little sex. That she was a tease, or worse, a prude.

She was none of those things. It was something else entirely. She might be inexperienced, but in her heart she knew once she had fully possessed and been possessed by Brad, it would be hard to let go.

And she had to let go. He was Brad Vandercamp. What was one week in his busy hop from one continent to another?

Thank God her brain had kicked in. Just in time to bring her crazy body to a halt!

Only what would happen now? Would the worldly, sophisticated Brad Vandercamp change his mind about wasting his holiday with a prudish, unsophisticated tease? He, who had his choice of far more interesting places, more glamorous women who wouldn't make such a big deal out of a night in the sack.

Her heart lurched. She turned to look at him. Not a glance this time, but a long, steady gaze. She would remember forever. The handsome, rugged profile, the always-rumpled hair that had the bright tawny color of a lion's coat, the readable hazel eyes that smiled, coaxed and promised. She looked at his hands on the wheel, strong hands that could be so gentle.

Please, God. I want this week. If I never have more. So far it has been such fun. More than fun. A happy togetherness that has somehow added more sparkle, joy and meaning to the things I've been doing all of my life.

But maybe... She swallowed, and her heart grew heavy as he pulled into the Ashford driveway. What they had been doing must have seemed rather dull and mundane to him. Perhaps he would rather—

"Well!" He turned to her, and he was smiling. "What's on the program for tomorrow?"

As it turned out, there were five others for Christmas dinner. No, not just for dinner. For the whole day. They had discussed the guest list earlier in the week while they baked Christmas goodies. Mostly he shelled nuts and helped decorate the cookies. Something else he had never done before.

"Why don't you invite Parker?" Paula suggested as she measured ingredients for ginger cookies. "I know he's a loner, but surely, on Christmas Day..."

"I already asked him," he said, sampling a sugar cookie still warm from the oven. "Delicious. He's coming."

"And Mr. Andrews, if he's still here."

"Still here and not wasting time."

"He's a dynamo, isn't he? I'm glad you decided to take him on."

"We decided," he said. He had brought Paula along for the dinner interview with Andrews. First time, except for that maid's outfit, he'd ever seen her in a dress. She had looked great in that simple black sheath, showing off those dynamite legs.

"What do you mean, we?"

"Well, maybe it was mostly you." He had been intrigued by her warm interest and the ease with which she drew the man out. "You were so busy digging into his personal life I didn't get a chance to check his qualifications."

"Oh, you! You had all that stuff on paper," she said, dumping the dough onto the board she had dusted with flour. "You wanted to know the man, didn't you?"

"Right." And he had learned all he needed to know in one short interview. She had handled Andrews as deftly as she was handling that cookie dough, he thought. The man had poured out his heart to them. His early retirement to care for an ailing wife. How her recent death had left him bereft and lost. And, yes, he would like to get back into business.

"Poor man," Paula said. "He needs to be busy."

"And I need his experience. We've already had a couple of long sessions with Parker and we're now zeroing in on prospective architects and contractors."

She smiled at him. "And you're rather enjoying it, aren't you?"

"It's interesting," he said. He had found himself drawn more deeply into the negotiations as Andrews brought up angles he should consider. And, yes, he was enjoying it. Perhaps he, too, needed to be busy.

Andrews accepted Brad's invitation. He drove out

early with Parker. They joined Lew, who declared, "Nothing like a hard jaunt on horseback to work up a good appetite."

Lew had brought Sam Jones, one of his poker cronies, along with him. "He's alone and a little down. Just got his pink slip from the navy base."

Jones, who had no taste for horses, declined the offer of a ride. "I'll keep Parker company. We'll just wander around on foot and take a look."

"I don't think he'll find Parker much company," Paula said before she retreated to the house for last-minute doings. "He looks like his mind is a mile away."

The other guest was Sid, one of Brad's stable boys, a nineteen-year-old who seemed to have no family connections. He said he would go in and "help Miss Paula."

Earlier, Brad had said to Paula that it seemed unfair all their guests were men and that she was doing all the work.

Paula said she was used to being overloaded with men. It was Mom's policy to invite every lonesome cowboy on the Randolph ranch to share Christmas with them. "And I won't be doing all the work. They'll pitch in."

She was right. *At least Sid is certainly pitching in,* Brad thought, watching the young man follow Paula about the kitchen. His efforts were rather clumsy as his eyes remained constantly and adoringly on Paula.

Paula didn't seem to notice. He remembered she was used to being overloaded with men. *And maybe,* he thought, with a sudden jolt of jealousy, *I'm just one of them.* That night he had wanted so desperately to make love with her, he had thought she felt the same way.

But maybe not. Hadn't she slipped easily into their casual routine? Just an occasional light kiss or a hug. Fewer of them, and lighter. A kind of touch-me, touch-me-not game, he thought with a grimace.

Something else he had never before experienced. Other women...

He stopped. Paula was Paula, unlike any other woman he had known.

He was trying to play by her rules, but he could hardly keep his hands off her. He wanted to take her in his arms and hold her there forever.

Forever.

That was the difference. There had been many women in his life. He had been interested, intrigued, once deeply infatuated. But never before had he thought about forever.

But how did Paula feel? There was something between them, something deeper than lust. He could have sworn she felt it, too. But, if so, how could she have so easily distanced herself? Subtly, perhaps, but she had drawn away. And Lew had made it clear that he thought Brad was not good enough for his niece.

Damn! Was he getting some kind of complex? He'd never felt so unsure, so...scared!

Bloody hell! He'd ask her right out. They needed to talk.

He strode across the kitchen. "Paula, I—"

"Watch it!" she warned, as she opened the oven.

He stepped back as the steam rose, and the succulent odor of roasting turkey that had permeated the room became more potent. He was not to be deterred. "Paula, I want to ask you something."

"And I want to ask you something," she said. "Can you carve a turkey?"

CHAPTER TWELVE

DIFFERENT place, different people. But definitely not all the same, Brad thought in the buzz of activity as everybody gathered for dinner.

No one was exquisitely clad. Ellis Andrews was the only one who had appeared in coat and tie, and he had discarded them to get on a horse.

No clicking of champagne glasses. No idle gossip, either. Everyone was too busy, as Paula had predicted, pitching in. That is, everyone except Lew, who was already seated and directing everybody else. Parker, also seated, seemed to be still locked in some world of his own. Probably mentally processing another world-shaking innovation, Brad conceded, as he poured wine.

Lew placed a hand over his glass. "I'll take beer."

"I don't think we have any," Brad said.

"In the fridge. I brought a six-pack."

Brad went to the kitchen for the beer, almost bumping into Sid, who, with Sam Jones, was helping Paula bring in the side dishes.

Soon they were all seated, and Ellis Andrews was carving the turkey. Brad knew he couldn't carve it today, even had he known how. He was too engrossed in what he wanted to say to Paula, who was seated directly across from him.

She had taken off that big apron and looked even more alluring in a simple but festive red sweater.

"Light or dark?" Andrew's voice rose sightly above the babble of voices. Brad heard and didn't hear. He wanted to walk around the table, take her in his arms and—

"Brad!"

A little startled, he turned to Andrews. "Yes?"

"What's your preference? Light or dark meat?"

"Oh...either, both." What did it matter what he ate? And what was wrong with him? How could he be as befuddled as young Sid?

He wasn't the bloody womanizer he was reputed to be, but he was...what had that American guy called him?

Smooth.

He smiled. Nothing smooth about trying to talk to a woman who was dealing with a hot roasting pan full of a heavy turkey.

Not the right setting to say I love you, but when you fell for a woman who hung around a kitchen, making dinner for a mob...

Love?

A word he'd never said to any woman. Or, like forever, never thought.

"You can do something about that, can't you, Brad?"

Brad gave Lew a blank stare. What was he talking about?

"Sam doesn't want to leave San Diego. Tell him." Lew nodded toward the man he had brought with him.

Brad turned to Sam Jones with a questioning look.

"Oh, I was just saying I hate to leave the area. But I guess I'll have to. Got my pink slip yesterday."

"Pink slip?" Brad asked, puzzled.

"Notice. Dismissed. No job," Lew explained.

"I see." Brad wondered how he could help. The man seemed to have a thing against horses, but—"What's your line?"

"Painting. A little carpentry. I've been on the maintenance crew at the base for the past year."

"Base?"

"Naval base. It's closing. So I'm one of the first to go...last hired, first fired."

"That's too bad."

"Oh, I'm better off than most. Hey, Paula, may I have a little more of that dressing?" he said, passing his plate. "Yeah, that's right, lots of that out-of-this-world gravy." When his plate was returned, he dug in with appreciation before turning to Brad. "I'm single and unshackled. I feel sorry for guys like my friend Tom. He's got four kids and just bought a new house. Gonna be hard for him to move, even if he can find another job somewhere."

"He'll have to move?"

"Are you kidding? Over twenty-six thousand people working at that base. Closing it is gonna cut a gap in this city's employment that'll leave it at zero! Tom, like most of us, is in trouble. Ain't many places to run to. Military bases all over the country closing like crazy. Guess we need another war."

"I'm afraid that wouldn't help," Ellis Andrews said. "It wouldn't require more people. Just more buttons to push." This prompted much laughter and some discussion about the pros and cons of the electronic age they were living in.

As Lew put it, "Nobody hires anybody to answer the damn phone."

"Well, I'm glad they can't push a button to hammer a nail or slap a paintbrush around. Not yet, anyway." Sam recited the dire circumstances of some base employees who had lost or were about to lose their jobs. An older man, five years away from retirement. A single mother with a Down's Syndrome child. "She don't want to move the kid away from this good program she's in, but if she loses the job that's paying for it..." Sam shook his head. "It's tough when you have your job pulled out from under you."

"Well, now, if you're talking about jobs, that's right down Brad's alley," Lew said, with a sidelong glance at Brad. "He's a Vandercamp."

"Huh?" Sam looked blank.

"Vandercamps don't sit on their money. They keep it working, making jobs for hundreds, thousands. Europe, Asia, anywhere...you name it. Piece of cake for Vandercamp Enterprises.''

Brad grinned. ''Rubbing my nose in it, Lew?''

''Your words. Not mine.''

''Well, they're fact. Not fancy,'' Brad said, stirred by a feeling so intense he could hardly contain himself. Something between anger and determination had hit him hard. It had nothing to do with Lew's goading. It was the thought of all those people, their lives and the burdens they shouldered, so dependent on the jobs they held. Jobs that could be snatched away in the blink of an eye.

All right, he was a Vandercamp. He knew about mergers and takeovers. He knew about millions made in the blink of an eye.

Now he was looking at it from the bottom side of the coin. He was repelled by the view.

By gad, he was a Vandercamp! ''Maybe we can dump a few jobs into San Diego. I'll check it out,'' he said, casually. But inside he was adamant. He wouldn't waste time. He wasn't a Vandercamp for nothing. Changes could be made in the blink of an eye.

It was a good Christmas, possibly the happiest of his life, he thought. But he grew restless as the evening progressed and nobody seemed anxious to leave. Appetites appeased, they sat around the cozy living room, comfortably relaxed, swapping jokes and laughing like they might stay forever. Then Paula, instead of hinting that the party was over, engaged them in a card game where each person put a penny in several pots, and you collected a certain pot if you had a certain card or won a certain sequence. She had even brought a stack of pennies to change for their dollars. Silly game, but it was fun. He could have enjoyed it as much as everybody else, even Lew, if he hadn't been so anxious to have Paula to himself.

The evening finally did come to an end. The men moved out, each loaded with a Christmas package of homemade cookies. Paula had been right, he conceded, when she told him she was not baking too many.

Thank goodness, he had engaged Dan's teenage daughter to do the cleanup. She came, accompanied by her boyfriend, before the men left. All he had to do was drag Paula out of the kitchen, where she was busy instructing them where to put things. For goodness sake, didn't she ever stop working?

"This is my kitchen, and they can put things where they please," he said, marching in. The giggles of the two young people echoed behind him as he strode out with Paula in his arms.

"Put me down!" she protested. "My goodness, what must they think?"

"I'll tell you what I think," he said, nuzzling her neck, loving the smell of her, a strange combination of freshly shampooed hair, that perfume she always wore and turkey dressing. "I think you think too much about what other people think." He didn't give a damn what anybody thought, as long as she was where he'd been aching to have her all day...in his arms. He touched his lips to hers and felt an instant response. Felt the unmistakable tremor of desire. "Ah, love," he whispered. "Let me please you."

"No. I... No." Even as her mouth sought his in begging surrender, she tried to withdraw.

Damn! His aching need for her was almost unbearable. He longed to carry her to his bed and hear her cry out in a passion of erotic pleasure as they came together.

"Please," she pleaded in a choked whisper. "Put me down."

It took all the willpower he possessed, but he let her slide to the floor. "Better take you home." He kissed her lightly on the temple and moved to collect her gifts from under the tree. *We need to talk,* he reminded himself. *We have to spell out whatever is between us.* But there was no privacy with those kids banging pans in the nearby kitchen.

She watched him, relief tempered by a keen sense of disappointment. It had been hard to hold him off all week. Tonight... She was still tingling with desire, ready to throw reservation to the wind.

Yes! One night with Brad would mean more to her than a lifetime with any other man. If all she was to have was now, this moment...

It wasn't too late. "Brad," she called softly.

"Ready?" He came toward her, loaded with packages. "I think I have them all."

She was jolted by a surge of anger. How could he be so calm, so composed while she... She couldn't help it. She was still shaking with an explosion of wild, tempestuous longing that he had awakened. While he...

"We're off!" he called to the kids in the kitchen, as he shifted the packages and took her arm.

Easy for him to turn off emotions. Like turning off a faucet, she thought. Face it—as easy as switching from one affair to another.

Well, she could be as cool, as sophisticated as he. To prove it, she kept up a continuous line of chatter as he maneuvered his way among the many cars on the freeway. She talked about the heavy traffic and how everybody must be coming or going to some Christmas party. She thought they all enjoyed theirs, even Parker, who came out of his world every now and then. Oh, and did she tell him how much she liked all the gifts? Though he shouldn't have given her so many. The cashmere sweater, so soft to the touch. And how had he remembered the book she wanted? But how could she tell him? "The diamond bracelet. It's lovely, but..."

"Shut up," he said, as he drove into the Ashford driveway and turned off the motor. "We need to talk."

"I am talking," she said, rather defiantly. She

didn't intend to discuss her reticence, prudishness, whatever he wanted to call it.

"I don't want to talk about trifles."

"There's nothing trifling about this bracelet." She fingered the delicate diamond chain encircling her wrist. She hadn't been able to resist wearing it one day, but it was far too expensive for her to accept. "Brad, it's lovely, but—"

He put his hand over hers. "I don't want to know what you think about the bracelet, Paula. I want to know what you think about me."

A lump rose in her throat, choking her. She ought to say, "I'm really fond of you," or "We have such fun together." Something like that. You didn't tell a man of many affairs that you were deeply in love with him.

She didn't trust herself to speak. But she couldn't help reaching up to tenderly brush his cheek, run a finger across his lips.

"Stop it!" He took her hand away, but held it tight in his. "I know about that."

"About what?" she asked, puzzled.

"The strong sexual attraction. And don't look at me like that! I'm not new at this sex game, Paula. I think you want me as much as I want you. But that's not what I'm talking about."

"What...what are you talking about, Brad?"

"I want to know how you really feel about me. If it even comes close to the way I feel."

"Which is?" she asked, holding her breath.

"I love you, Paula."

She stared at him, wondering if she had heard right. Wondering how many times he must have said that to how many—

"All right. I have a reputation. But I want you to know I've never said that to anyone before. And I don't even know when it happened. Maybe that first night when I saw you dancing while you worked. And maybe that's it, that practical hardworking, down-to-earth Cinderella that you are, combined with that bubbling enthusiasm about whatever you're doing, working or wishing on stars or warm and eager in my arms or... Bloody hell, why are you crying?"

"It's...oh, you love me. I never imagined that. I thought—"

"Well, it's nothing to cry about. And you still haven't said. How do you feel about me, Paula?"

"I love you, love you, love you too much. I was ready to settle for anything. A week, a day or just one night," she said with fervor.

"How about forever?" He leaned across to whisper against her lips.

"Let's go in and talk about it," she said. She hated these seats with the barrier between them.

They settled comfortably in the Ashford living room, but there was no talking for a long time.

It was Brad who finally spoke of details. He wanted to marry as soon as possible. Here or at her home in Wyoming? And where would she like to honeymoon? What about flying to Monaco, boarding the *Renegade* to cruise the Riviera? They could spend the latter part of January at the family's Italian villa.

Paula, seated on the sofa, snuggled in Brad's arms, smiled at him. "You know I couldn't do that. I'll be in school."

"School?" he asked, as if she had spoken in a foreign tongue.

"Back in session on the third," she said. "Oh, and that's when the Ashfords are due back. I'll have to give them notice, so I guess we couldn't get married until—"

"The hell with the Ashfords. You're through working."

"Well…" She hated to leave the Ashfords in the lurch, but perhaps something could be—

"The hell with school, too. Time for love and marriage, sweetheart."

"Yes, I know, but…" Give up school? Just when she was on the verge of becoming a doctor of veterinary science? Her lifelong dream. "Brad, I…I have to think about this."

"Nothing to think about, love. Do you think that when Cinderella married the prince, she kept shoveling ashes?"

"Ashes?" she mimicked with a hot flash of temper. "Is that what you think of my profession?"

"Oh, honey, don't get touchy. All right. It's a great profession. But not for you. To tell you the truth, I've been a little leery, anyway, about your handling horses.''

"I've handled horses all my life!"

"Riding them is one thing, but doctoring on them. They're... Hell, Paula, you're much too small. That's a man's job."

"Oh? You know a man as big as a horse?"

"Well..." He hesitated, and she knew that had stumped him.

"Or maybe you think I'm not as smart as a man!"

"I don't think anything of the kind. I don't know how we got into this, anyway."

"We got into it because you're discounting my whole life. This is something I have dreamed about, worked for all my life, and you think I can drop it like a hot poker just when I'm almost there!"

"Right!" Brad's temper rose to match hers. "I do want you to drop it. Working seems to be all you have been doing. I want you to stop and enjoy yourself. I want to give you things you've never had, show you places you've never seen. Love you, play games with you."

"I don't want to spend my life making love and playing games. That might be enough for you, but not for me!"

Brad gave her a look of utter amusement. Then he turned and walked out. She heard his car door slam, the engine whine and the squeal of the wheels as he sped away.

CHAPTER THIRTEEN

"WHAT'S the matter, Paula?" Lew asked, looking up from his breakfast.

"Too hot!" Paula fanned a hand against her mouth and quickly set down her coffee mug.

"Don't give me that. What's wrong?"

"Wrong?" She tried to look puzzled.

"Yeah, I want to know what it is. What's going on?"

"Same old, same old, as far as I'm concerned. How're the eggs?"

"Eggs fine like always. 'Cept you ain't eating any. So what's eating you?"

"Honestly, Lew, you are the limit!" Paula got up, poured out her coffee and slammed her mug into the dishwasher. "You think you know everything even when there's nothing to know!"

"I know doom and gloom when I see it, specially from a gal who's usually singing and bubbling all over the place. I know when a guy who's been haunting the place has been missing for two whole days. I know—"

"All right! All right!" She turned and glared at him. "If you must know, he dumped me!"

"Oh?"

"You said he would, didn't you!"

"Me?"

"You. I quote, 'I know these rich playboy types. They butter up a girl till they get tired of her and dump her like she's trash.'"

"Well, now... Wouldn't be the first time I've had to eat my words," Lew said, grinning.

The grin did it. Or was it what she said, which wasn't the way it was at all? Anyway, she couldn't stop her lips from quivering, her eyes filling.

He pointed to her chair. "Sit down. Talk to me."

She sat, but was too muddled to speak. Brad had said... Or was it she?

"To begin with, I'll say something." Lew pushed back his chair and turned to her. "I've seen that guy looking at you, and it wasn't like you was trash."

"No. I...I shouldn't have said that."

"What happened?"

"He...oh, Lew, he asked me to marry him." She lifted a hand to brush away the spilling tears.

"That's something to cry about?"

"That's just what he said. But I was so surprised, and the way he asked me... I had been trying, well, not to let things get out of hand, so I tried to...well, to keep my feelings under control. I guess I didn't do a very good job, because he said he knew I was anxious to go to bed with him but he wanted more than a night in the sack. I don't blame you for laughing. I had thought that was all he wanted. But...oh, Lew, he loves me, really loves me. He just wanted to be sure that what I felt for him was real. It is. I love him."

"So what happened?"

"I don't know." She hesitated. "Well, yes I do. Brad started talking about when and where we would get married and about a honeymoon cruise on his yacht and a few weeks at a villa in Italy."

"Sounds nice."

"Well, yes. But he was making all these plans like what I was doing didn't mean squat. My plans could be scotched. Bam! Just like that."

"School, huh?"

"More than school. Do you know that in just six months, I'll become a clinician?"

"What's that?"

"An intern, like in medicine."

"I see."

"Well, don't say it like it's nothing. It's what I have been planning all my life. You know how Toby and I planned, even when we were children. He was going to train racehorses, and I—"

"Things change, honey. Now Toby's a banker, and you're on your own."

"Darn right, I'm on my own! And I'm making it on my own. In one year, I'll be a licensed veterinarian. My own profession, something nobody can take from me. Independent."

"Are you scared?"

"Scared? What do you mean?"

"You were pretty hurt when Toby broke off. All you had to cling to was this goal, this profession.'"

"My goodness, Lew, you can't think I'm still pining for Toby. That was—"

"No. I don't think that. But I think what happened then makes you hold onto what was left when the going got tough. Call it a goal, work, independence...whatever. More like insurance. Something to hold onto if all else fails."

Was she afraid? Did she think that what was between Brad and herself was so frail it couldn't last? Brad's words came back, reminding her. Their love was real, far deeper than passion. Anyway, she knew she would take the risk whatever the cost.

"It's not anything like that, Lew," she said, explaining to herself, as well. "I've always loved animals, especially horses. You know that. I've always worked with them, and I don't want to stop now that I'm almost where I can really be of help. And...oh, I guess it's more than that. I want to be me! I want to do something."

"You'll always be you, honey. There's not an ounce of shallow do-nothing blood in you."

"But Brad wants to do for me, give me...so much. I—"

"Let him. You've always been such a giver yourself, always working, doing for somebody else...me, your ma, the Ashfords or anybody else who needs a hand, that you don't know how to take. Brad loves you. He wants to give to you."

"But...so much. It's overwhelming. Oh, I don't want to become just another shallow do-nothing society show-off like Whitney and that crowd."

"No danger of that. You're still you. As Brad's wife, you'd be—"

"Making love and playing games. Like I told him, that might be enough for him, but not for me."

Lew emitted a sharp whistle. "Boy! That ticked him off!"

She nodded, feeling miserable. "That's when he took off. But...how did you know?"

"Well, I kinda hinted at that myself. Hell, I didn't hint. Told him what I thought about a guy who didn't do nothing but sit on his money or the backside of a horse."

"So you know what I mean."

"I know what made him mad." Lew chuckled. "He came at me like a bucking bronco!"

Paula sighed. "He didn't come at me. He was too mad."

"Can't blame him, can you? We ain't got no cause to look down on him just 'cause he's rich. Gotta strip off the money and look at the man." Lew paused, thinking. "Guess I really seen him that night. Not 'cause he lit into me about that Vandercamp money. It was Parker. He looked like some no-good bum. Brad didn't know him from Adam, but he was ready to empty his pockets for him...not that there was much in his pockets," Lew added, with a hearty laugh. "Then, even while he was trying to convince me he was good enough for you, his mind was on the bum. Gave him his card. I could see his mind working...'The man needs a job.' Yep, that's when I decided Brad was an all-right guy."

Paula's heart warmed as Lew went on. "He was right about the Vandercamp money. Didn't you notice Christmas night how he listened to everything Sam said? I could see him feeling for the people Sam talked about. I'll bet you a dollar to a doughnut, he's going to put that money to work at the naval base. It's called business. But it's a powerful lot of giving to a whole lot of people."

High praise, she thought, from one who had been so skeptical. "What are you telling me, Lew?"

"I ain't telling you nothing. I'm asking. That horse your dad give you, Spitfire...you love him more'n you love Brad?"

"What! Don't be ridiculous. Brad means more to me than a horde of horses!"

"Well?"

"Oh, you! You're so...so street smart!"

"Yeh." He reached into his pocket to hand her something.

"What's that?"

"Key to the truck. I'd hate to see you let a good man get away."

Too choked up to speak, she took the key, started out. Turned to give Lew a spontaneous hug. "I'm glad you're my godfather," she said, and kissed the top of his head before rushing out.

Bradley Elmwood Vandercamp, Senior, put down his cup and glared at his son. "That's the worst cup of coffee I've ever tasted."

Brad lifted his shoulders in apology. "I haven't got the hang of it yet."

"Haven't got a cook, either, I see. Housekeeper? Nobody."

"Didn't get around to that yet." Paula wasn't ready for a staff. Too used to doing everything herself, he thought. He'd give her time. *Whatever she wants. I'm not about to let her walk out of my life.*

You were the one who walked, chum!

Well, I'm walking back! She'll have to give me time, too.

His father broke into his trance. "You'd better get around to it soon. Most inconvenient without help. This coffee—"

"Sorry. I didn't expect you so soon." His father had been enthusiastic when he called about the base. "I'd like to see it. I'm also rather curious about this little place you've bought, son." Two days later, here he was.

"Wanted to catch you while you were in the mood," he said now.

"Me? Mood? What are you talking about?"

"Business." His father smiled, but his expression

was serious. "Are you ready to join Vandercamp Enterprises?"

"Oh. I hadn't thought…"

"Second time this month you've consulted me about some big project. Some scanning device, and now this base."

"Oh. Parker's a long story. But that's quite a device he has. Then later I was talking to Sam. He works at the base, was concerned about it closing, and I thought you might have some ideas."

Bradley Vandercamp, Senior, nodded. "People and ideas. That's business, son."

"And I'm beginning to get a kick out of it," Brad said. Quite a challenge, he thought, working business from the bottom side of the coin. "Yes. I'd like to become a working part of Vandercamp Enterprises."

"Good. We need fresh blood. Armstrong came along with me. He's at the hotel and will take a look at the base before we decide to bid." He had already told Brad that Armstrong, a British movie producer, was looking for a studio site in the States.

"Would he need all that space?" Brad asked, feeling anxious. "And what about the current workers?"

"Are you kidding? Every bit of the space. And he'd certainly retain most, maybe all of the employees. You see…" He broke off at the sound of a car door. Someone ran up the steps and across the porch.

Light, familiar footsteps. Brad rose and rushed from the kitchen.

He met her in the hall. Their simultaneous apologies were mumbled and lost in a storm of fervent kisses as he enfolded her in his arms.

It was some time before he led her into the kitchen. "Father," he said, an unmistakable ring of pride in his voice. "I'd like you to meet Paula, the woman I love and hope to marry." He gave Paula a questioning look, but she was looking at his father.

She swallowed as the distinguished gentleman politely rose and looked at her. She would have liked to be at her best when she met Brad's parents. Not in these old jeans and pullover. And had she combed her hair? What must he think of her?

There was nothing but astonishment in his expression as he politely held out his hand, but whatever he was going to say was interrupted by Sid. He rushed in, the screen door banging behind him.

"Dan wants you to come quick, Mr. Brad," he said. "It's Caspar."

"What's wrong?" Brad asked.

"Don't know. Maybe pneumonia, Dan thinks. But it's real bad."

Paula was already heading for the truck. Caspar was the most prized of Brad's polo ponies. Brad and his father joined her, and they followed Sid, who was on horseback.

Dan had isolated Caspar in one of the smaller corrals. Paula climbed over the fence and rushed to his side. Her heart sank as she looked at the great beast. He stood as if his hoofs were rooted to the ground, and never had she seen such labored breathing. His great rib cage rose and fell, his mouth gaped wide, and his eyes looked as if they might burst from his head in wild terror.

This was not pneumonia. The horse was frantically battling to get some air into his lungs.

She heard the anxious voices of the men around her. "Vet's on his way," she heard Dan say. "If he can only last."

But Paula knew he couldn't last long. What was wrong? She strained to recall all she had learned.

She looked at the foam bubbling from his mouth and the flaring nostrils.

Anthrax?

She hadn't noticed any vegetation that would carry the infectious bacilli, but...

She ran a hand along the flank and was relieved to find none of the ugly round pustules. The hide was smooth but unusually warm. If she only had her thermometer.

She had nothing, and she didn't know what was wrong.

Poor Caspar. She could hardly bear the agonized panting. In helpless despair, she rested her cheek against his neck, wishing... Jerked back from the scorching heat. Yes, this hot!

She looked up. A shaft of sun glared in her face. Touched a chord.

She spun to face Dan. "You exercised him this morning?"

He nodded. "Quite a long session. He seemed all right then. It was only after—"

"Sunstroke!" she said, not waiting for him to finish. "Hook up a water hose. Quick!" she called to Sid.

In moments it was done, and she focused a steady stream of the blessed cold water on the horse. She sprayed the cooling jet over every inch of the huge form, face, neck, ribs and legs.

Prayed.

It seemed longer, but it must have been about five minutes later that she heard Caspar gulp, slightly move his head.

"By golly, he's coming round," Dan said.

Yes, Paula thought, weak with relief when Caspar shook himself and turned his head. Like watching a miracle, she saw his distress diminish as his breathing became easier.

Paula was only vaguely aware of the murmurs of awed satisfaction and relief. But she heard Brad loud and clear. "You've done it, my love. You saved his life. Here, let me help."

She leaned against him as he took the hose from her. They laughed as they watched the beloved horse rock his head back and forth and open his mouth to the spray, relishing the healing water.

It was forty-five minutes later that the vet from the university veterinary hospital arrived. "I would have been too late to save him," he said. He advised Dan to carefully monitor the exercise and time outdoors for all the horses. "The weather is unusually hot for December, even in this area."

"El Niño," Mr Vandercamp said. "Isn't that the term given this strange phenomenon that's causing such an upheaval in climatic conditions all over the world?"

"Yes," the vet agreed. "And you were lucky to have one of our brightest students at hand." He was on the teaching staff and well acquainted with Paula.

"It was clever of you to recognize sunstroke and act on it at once," he told her. "That was quick thinking."

"But it wasn't quick thinking," she told Brad much later when everyone had departed, and they were finally alone together. "What I did today was due to a long memory and James Herriot."

"The Scottish vet who wrote those—"

"Wonderful, funny, beautiful books!" she finished. "Every word is stamped on my brain, and today, just when I needed it, something surfaced."

"Oh?"

"It was almost like magic, Brad. In the book, it was not a horse, but a bull. Nobody, not even Herriot, could figure out what was wrong. Anyway, today, when I touched Caspar and he was so hot, it all came back to me. The way he was standing and trying to catch his breath. Every symptom was the same as the bull in the book. So I just did what Herriot did for the bull. And it worked!"

"It certainly did," Brad said. "Did I remember to thank you?"

"You did."

"Did I tell you that I love you?"

"And I love you," she said, throwing her arms around him. "More than anything. We can be married as soon as you like, go away whenever and wherever—"

"Hey, what brought this on?"

"Lew. He really lectured me this morning. You're quite a person, according to him."

"You're kidding. Are you referring to the same Lew I know?"

She chuckled. "I certainly am. It was his idea that I should come out here today. Said I shouldn't let a good man get away."

"How about that! I owe him more than twelve dollars."

"Twelve dollars?" she asked, puzzled.

"Never mind. Let's talk about what's important. Do you think I'll let you abandon your profession after today's performance?"

"You mean you'd let me keep on with school and we'd get married later and—"

"I mean we'll get married as soon as possible. We'll remain here while you're in school or until you're ready to move on."

She could hardly contain her joy. But… "Are you

sure you want to do that?" A man accustomed to moving from one faraway place to another...

"Did I tell you that for the first time in my life, I feel that I've come home?"

"Oh, Brad!" It was all she could say.

"It's not the place, love. It's you."

"And mine is with you," she said. "Only... You're making all the compromises. I'm to have both my profession and you. Is that fair?"

"Not to worry. I'm starting a profession of my own, part of which will be conducted here. Tell you about it later. And as for being fair...don't get too complacent. There's another old saying, a bit of advice I'm considering. Something about keeping her barefoot and pregnant."

She didn't know whether to laugh or slap him. Anyway, she couldn't do either while she was being smothered with kisses.

EPILOGUE

PAULA sat beside Mr. Vandercamp in the recently acquired Vandercamp box at the exclusive Green Acres polo field. Today's game, her first, was the Silver Cup, traditionally played every New Year's Day for the benefit of crippled children. She was entranced from the beginning, when the players, all neat and trim in their uniforms, rode out, lining up in teams. An impressive scene, but her eyes were glued to one man—Brad, correctly attired in white riding britches, blue stripes on his white polo shirt and matching helmet. His brown English boots hugged Caspar's flanks, and he looked so strikingly handsome astride the great beast that her heart turned over.

"He looks so poised and regal," she said. "No wonder they call him the polo prince!"

Mr. Vandercamp smiled. "No, my dear. It's his command of the game that earned that title," he said.

She supposed that was true as she watched him play, skillful and alert in all that confusion of racing horses, men and whacking mallets.

But she could hardly keep up with the game, no

matter how patiently Mr. Vandercamp explained. Still, she found it exciting.

"Amazing," she told Mr. V. "How the horses seem to sense what to do."

"Polo ponies are a special breed all their own," he said. "Combining the special skills of all the great breeds, from the speed of a racehorse to the intelligence of an Arabian."

"You're right," she said, even more impressed by the performance of the ponies as the game progressed.

She was so excited. She watched each move, each play.

She never noticed that someone was watching her.

"It is Paula, Mama," Whitney insisted.

"Don't be ridiculous. Paula's at the house. Or should be," she added, frowning. "I can't understand why she wasn't there when we arrived!"

"She wasn't expecting us until day after tomorrow," Rae reminded her.

"Of course!" Whitney snapped. "It was only after Sheila called and told us Brad would be playing today that we cut our visit short. So Paula thought she had a chance to do whatever she pleased!"

"But what on earth would she be doing here?" Mrs. Ashford asked.

"Oh, she's a pushy little show-off!" Whitney said. "What I'd like to know is where she got that gorgeous outfit and how she managed to hook up with a man who has access to a box."

"She's seated in a box? All the boxes are full. At least Sally's was too full for us," Mrs. Ashford exclaimed, picking up her opera glasses to peer at the row of boxes far below them. "I don't see how—" She broke off with a gasp. "Good heavens! I think you're right. It is Paula. How on earth…?"

The game was over and the crowd dispersing. Paula remained in her seat, sipping champagne and talking with Mr. Vandercamp as they waited for Brad to join them. The Ashford trio was still some distance away when she spotted them coming toward her.

Oh, dear, she thought, *I haven't had time to explain. I told Brad I would have to give her notice, time to find another maid, and I will. But now…*

"Paula!" Mrs. Ashford stood before her, her voice sharp and demanding. "What are you doing here?"

"I…I came to see the game. Mrs. Ashford, I'd like you to meet—"

The introduction was intercepted by Whitney. "You've no business here! You should be at your job! I couldn't find what I wanted to wear, and I needed you to fix my hair."

"I am so sorry. But you seem to have managed. You look quite presentable, Whitney."

Whitney, looking more miffed than pleased by this remark, was about to retort when Brad vaulted over the box railing to join them. "Oh, Brad, you were terrific!" she cried, turning from Paula to rush toward him. "You made me so proud! I must reward you," she added, lifting inviting lips.

Brad stepped back, avoiding her kiss and intended embrace by capturing both her hands in his. "Thank you, Whitney, but it was a team victory. So glad you enjoyed the game." He repeated his thanks to Mrs. Ashford and Rae, who also came forward with congratulations. An introduction to his father incited another flutter of admiration.

"Oh, I am so very happy to meet you," Mrs. Ashford said, gushing. "I have heard so much about our momentous accomplishments and your beautiful estate, Balmour." She was about to say more, but her recital came to an abrupt halt when she saw Brad's arm encircle Paula's waist.

"Has Paula told you the good news?" he asked.

Mrs. Ashford gaped, but she couldn't seem to speak.

It was Rae who asked, "What news?"

"Paula has consented to marry me," Brad said.

"But she can't!" The words seemed to explode involuntarily from Whitney. "You can't have met.... I mean, how can you know her? She's our maid. She should be—"

"Shut up, Whitney!" Mamie Ashford's shout was a stinging whiplash, cutting off Whitney's babbling.

Whitney, mouth agape, stared at her mother.

Mamie Ashford took no notice. Her attention was on Paula, her eyes gleaming in a practical grasp of the situation. "Oh, Paula, my dear, my dear! How perfectly wonderful!" She gave Paula a loving kiss before turning to Mr. Vandercamp. "She's part of our family, you know. Like another daughter. My, my, we'll have to get busy preparing for the wedding. It must be from our house, and Rae and Whitney will be bridesmaids. Like sisters, they are, you know. Just think, girls! Your sister, Paula, will be a Vandercamp, living at Balmour, among all those lords...and ladies, of course. And when we visit, we'll have such fun. Oh, my, we must never let our dear Paula be far from us."

MILLS & BOON®

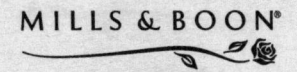

Next Month's Romance Titles

Each month you can choose from a wide variety of romance novels from Mills & Boon®. Below are the new titles to look out for next month from the Presents...™ and Enchanted™ series.

Presents...™

A CONVENIENT BRIDEGROOM	Helen Bianchin
IRRESISTIBLE TEMPTATION	Sara Craven
THE BAD GIRL BRIDE	Jennifer Drew
MISTRESS FOR A NIGHT	Diana Hamilton
A TREACHEROUS SEDUCTION	Penny Jordan
ACCIDENTAL BABY	Kim Lawrence
THE BABY GAMBIT	Anne Mather
A MAN TO MARRY	Carole Mortimer

Enchanted™

KIDS INCLUDED!	Caroline Anderson
PARENTS WANTED!	Ruth Jean Dale
MAKING MR RIGHT	Val Daniels
A VERY PRIVATE MAN	Jane Donnelly
LAST-MINUTE BRIDEGROOM	Linda Miles
DR. DAD	Julianna Morris
DISCOVERING DAISY	Betty Neels
UNDERCOVER BACHELOR	Rebecca Winters

On sale from 6th August 1999

H1 9907

Available at most branches of WH Smith, Tesco, Asda, Martins, Borders, Easons, Volume One/James Thin and most good paperback bookshops

THE Regency COLLECTION
Where rogues find romance

Look out for the fourth volume in this limited collection of Regency Romances from Mills & Boon® in August.

Featuring:

The Outrageous Dowager
by Sarah Westleigh

and

Devil-May-Dare
by Mary Nichols

Still only £4.99

MILLS & BOON®
Makes any time special™

Available at most branches of WH Smith, Tesco, Martins, Borders, Easons, Volume One/James Thin and most good paperback bookshops

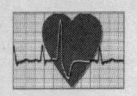

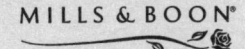

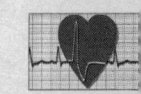

MILLS & BOON®
Medical Romance™

COMING NEXT MONTH from 6th August

ONE IN A MILLION by Margaret Barker
Bundles of Joy

Sister Tessa Grainger remembered Max Forster when he arrived as consultant on her Obs and Gynae ward, for she'd babysat when his daughter Francesca was small. But Max wasn't the carefree man she'd known. Tessa wanted him to laugh again and—maybe—even love again...

POLICE SURGEON by Abigail Gordon

Dr Marcus Owen was happy to be a GP and Police Surgeon, until he found one of the practice partners was Caroline Croft, the woman he'd once loved. Caroline was equally dismayed, for she still loved Marcus! Brought back together by their children, where did they go from here?

IZZIE'S CHOICE by Maggie Kingsley

Sister Isabella Clark came back to discover a new broom A&E consultant, but being followed around by Ben Farrell ended with her speaking her mind and Ben apologised! Since he liked her "honesty", Izzie kept it up, but it wasn't until the hospital fête that they realised they might have something more...

THE HUSBAND SHE NEEDS by Jennifer Taylor
A Country Practice #4

When District Nurse Abbie Fraser hears that Nick Delaney is home, she isn't sure how she feels, for Nick is now in a wheelchair. Surely she can make Nick see he has a future? But at what cost to herself, when she realises she has never stopped loving him?

Available at most branches of WH Smith, Tesco, Asda, Martins, Borders, Easons, Volume One/James Thin and most good paperback bookshops

MILLS & BOON

Historical Romance™

Coming next month

LADY JANE'S PHYSICIAN
by Anne Ashley
A Regency Delight

Lady Jane Beresford visited her cousin, but her enjoyment was marred by meeting Dr Thomas Carrington. Tom's blunt attitudes irritated Jane out of her own good manners! But he knew, if she didn't, that an Earl's daughter was far above his touch...

UNTAMED HEART
by Georgina Devon
A Regency delight! Book 1 of 3

Lizabeth Johnstone was shocked by her primitive reaction to Lord Alastair St. Simon. He should be every woman's dream, but he wasn't *hers* for Alastair was responsible for her younger's brother's death. Her stubborn refusal to accept help left him with only one alternative—they'd have to get married...

On sale from 6th August 1999

Available at most branches of WH Smith, Tesco, Asda, Martins, Borders, Easons, Volume One/James Thin and most good paperback bookshops

MILLS & BOON®
Makes any time special™

By Request

Bestselling themed romances brought back to you by popular demand

Each month By Request brings you three full-length novels in one beautiful volume featuring the best of the best.

So if you missed a favourite Romance the first time around, here is your chance to relive the magic from some of our most popular authors.

**Look out for
Passion in August 1999
featuring Michelle Reid,
Miranda Lee and Susan Napier**

*Available at most branches of WH Smith, Tesco,
Asda, Martins, Borders, Easons,
Volume One/James Thin
and most good paperback bookshops*

4 FREE
books and a surprise gift!

We would like to take this opportunity to thank you for reading this Mills & Boon® book by offering you the chance to take FOUR more specially selected titles from the Enchanted™ series absolutely FREE! We're also making this offer to introduce you to the benefits of the Reader Service™—

- ★ FREE home delivery
- ★ FREE gifts and competitions
- ★ FREE monthly Newsletter
- ★ Exclusive Reader Service discounts
- ★ Books available before they're in the shops

Accepting these FREE books and gift places you under no obligation to buy, you may cancel at any time, even after receiving your free shipment. Simply complete your details below and return the entire page to the address below. *You don't even need a stamp!*

YES! Please send me 4 free Enchanted books and a surprise gift. I understand that unless you hear from me, I will receive 6 superb new titles every month for just £2.40 each, postage and packing free. I am under no obligation to purchase any books and may cancel my subscription at any time. The free books and gift will be mine to keep in any case.

N9EA

Ms/Mrs/Miss/Mr ....Initials....................................
BLOCK CAPITALS PLEASE
Surname ....
Address ....
....
....Postcode...................................

Send this whole page to:
THE READER SERVICE, FREEPOST CN81, CROYDON, CR9 3WZ
(Eire readers please send coupon to: P.O. BOX 4546, DUBLIN 24.)

Offer valid in UK and Eire only and not available to current Reader Service subscribers to this series. We reserve the right to refuse an application and applicants must be aged 18 years or over. Only one application per household. Terms and prices subject to change without notice. Offer expires 31st Janaury 2000. As a result of this application, you may receive further offers from Harlequin Mills & Boon and other carefully selected companies. If you would prefer not to share in this opportunity please write to The Data Manager at the address above.

Mills & Boon is a registered trademark owned by Harlequin Mills & Boon Limited.
Enchanted is being used as a trademark.

Bestselling author

LAURA VAN WORMER
WEST END

where the people who report the news...
are the news

From its broadcast centre in Manhattan,
DBS—TV's newest network—is making
headlines. Beyond the cameras, the
careers of the industry's brightest stars
are being built.

MIRA®

Published 18th June 1999